D IS FOR DRESS-UP

Also by Alison Tyler

———

Best Bondage Erotica

Best Bondage Erotica 2

Exposed

Got a Minute?

The Happy Birthday Book of Erotica

Heat Wave: Sizzling Sex Stories

Luscious: Stories of Anal Eroticism

The Merry XXXmas Book of Erotica

Red Hot Erotica

Slave to Love

Three-Way

Caught Looking (with Rachel Kramer Bussel)

A is for Amour

B is for Bondage

C is for Coeds

D IS FOR DRESS-UP

EROTIC STORIES
EDITED BY ALISON TYLER

CLEIS
PRESS

Published in the United States by Cleis Press Inc.,
P.O. Box 14697, San Francisco, California 94114.

Printed in the United States.
Cover design: Scott Idleman
Text design: Karen Quigg
Cleis Press logo art: Juana Alicia
First Edition.
10 9 8 7 6 5 4 3 2 1

ACKNOWLEDGMENTS

Deepest Divine Distinction goes to:

Adam Nevill

Barbara Pizio

Felice Newman

Frédérique Delacoste

Diane Levinson

Violet Blue

and SAM, always.

Clothes make the man. Naked people have little or no influence on society.

—MARK TWAIN

contents

INTRODUCTION

DREAM WITH ME. Dream of closets filled with fantasy outfits…
schoolgirl skirts, high-heeled leather boots, shimmering prom
gowns, slippery latex slacks. Oh, and, of course, accessories: velvet
gloves, fishnet stockings, lacy rose-adorned garters, silky scarlet knickers.

Now, dream a little more. Of a collection of stories featuring those
same types of fantasy attire, a whole walk-in closet filled to overflow-
ing with decadent tales. That was my dream when I put out a call for
this collection. I didn't assign outfits to the authors. Instead, I was
much more interested in what "playing dress-up" meant to them.

To me, dressing up doesn't mean donning high-heeled shoes and
a fancy gown. Doesn't *always* mean that, anyway. Dressing up is what
I do every single day. Sliding on a different costume, depending on my
mood. Some days, you'll find me in jeans and a man's-style bowling
shirt featuring someone else's name on the pocket. Other days, I need

a schoolgirl skirt to feel complete. Check me out in my shiny penny loafers, opaque hose, and cashmere cardigan.

But dressing up inspires different things in different people. Some focus on the outerwear, like the uptight boyfriend in Tenille Brown's story "Presenting Paulette," who dresses his lady to look like his mother. Others notice only undergarments, like the narrator in Thomas S. Roche's "French Cut." Sometimes shoes are all that matter—drool over Shanna Germain's fantastic fantasy footwear in "Puss-in-Boots." And sometimes a true head-to-toe makeover is required for a sexy change, such as Rachel Kramer Bussel's "Dorothy for the Day."

Bryn Haniver's narrator makes short work of an old prom dress in "Rags to Riches," while a trip to a costume shop is necessary for the character in Michelle Houston's story, "A Long-Held Fantasy."

From slinky undergarments to the finishing touch of lipstick (lose yourself in Tsaurah Litzky's unexpected treasure), you'll find them all in *D Is for Dress-Up*. Now, open wide this fantasy closet, and reach inside…

XXX,
Alison Tyler

CLARE MOORE

SHE KNEW

EEP DOWN, SHE KNEW she was going to get screwed.

She'd helped him pick out his clothes for his new job. She'd helped with three jackets and five pairs of pants, and about six shirts. He had been back a couple of times in the last two weeks. She'd helped him put on and take off jackets. She'd measured his inseam and his shoulders and his chest.

On his third visit, he didn't bother going into the dressing room to change pants. He just dropped them there in front of her, and stood in his tight boxers. It was probably then that she went a little higher in his crotch when he was trying on another pair of pants. She touched his balls with the back of her hand, and kept on measuring.

He began to get bigger, and he turned away, embarrassed.

He paid for his selections, and asked her out, for Friday after the shop closed; for tonight. She knew she was going to get screwed. She thought about it all day. She thought about when it would happen, and where. She thought about what she should wear, so it would be easy for him, with a simple dress that would lift over her head in a flash, showing maybe a black lace bra.

Maybe a soft satin blouse with a hundred buttons, so that it would take forever to open her up, with only a T under it. She hadn't decided, when she dressed in the morning, and now had only about an hour before he would walk in the door.

You had to wear the right clothes for a first screw. It was just a matter of how much time it should take and how hard it should be to get there. The last customer had long since left. She had to decide.

By the time the bell rang over the door as he walked in, she was ready. She was standing in the middle of the three dressing mirrors, so he saw her from front, back, and sides. She stood with her hands on her hips and her legs apart, in a mannequin pose.

He stopped when he saw her and crossed his arms as he stood there and took her in from bottom to top.

Brown wingtip shoes with black over-the-calf socks.

Very snug pleated and creased dark blue trousers with a faint pinstripe.

No belt.

Dark blue suspenders, buttoned to her pants, and tight against her chest.

A matching blue double-breasted jacket, buttoned.

A thin elegant white striped shirt, buttoned up to her neck.

A tight white armless striped undershirt, over her bare breasts.

And a silk blue-and-maroon print tie, properly knotted, hanging down her front.

No bra. And silk boxers. Black.

She was going to get screwed, but wanted it different. And wanted it to take time. He walked up to her. She pulled closed the curtain in front of the mirrors. She reached into her inside breast pocket and took out a deck of cards. She held them out to him in the palm of her hand.

He cut the deck. 7.

She cut it. 4.

She took off her jacket. One hardened nipple slipped from behind the suspenders, and pushed out the shirt.

He cut again. 10.

She. Jack.

She removed his jacket for him and hung it on the hook. It was one she had sold him.

Next, his belt. He insisted it was not part of his pants.

Her shoes.

Her socks.

His tie, his shoes, his socks.

He cut. King!

Ace!

He started to unbutton his shirt. She unfastened his pants instead. He dropped them and stepped out of them. He was bulging in his boxers. It was down to his boxers and shirt. She still had her tie, suspenders, shirt, pants, and underwear.

His shirt!

He took the deck and shuffled it. He stepped back off the platform and sat in the dressing room chair, in only his boxers. He drew a card, not looking at it, and tossed it toward her. It landed on the platform face up. 3.

He drew another card and, without looking at it, held it up for her to see. 5.

He got up, went to her, and undid her tie, brushing against her breasts as he removed it.

He went back to the chair and tossed her a 9. He held up a Queen. He pointed to her pants. She pointed to her suspenders, shrugged, and slipped them to her sides. Both nipples were hard.

8. 9. She started to unbutton her shirt, slowly, pulled it out of her pants, then pulled the shirt open to reveal her breasts and slipped the shirt off. He started throbbing in his boxers.

She walked over to him and drew a card. Ace. He drew. Ace! He held the deck to her. She slowly shook her head, and unfastened and dropped her pants. She stepped back and pointed to the mirrored platform.

He walked to it, shaking his head. Facing the mirrors, he slid his boxers down and kicked them off the platform. He didn't turn around. She could see him, erect, from three views. He shook his head and put his hands on his hips, and turned around, stepping off the platform.

He drew one last card. The fourth Ace. He held it up for her to see. She knew she was going to get screwed. She knew it was going to be now. He slipped off her silk boxers and grabbed her in his arms, and pushed her back against the mirrors, and thrust himself into her.

SaSKIa WaLKeR

SKIN ON SKIN

"**D**EEP BREATHS," Jade whispered to herself, as she attempted to quell her erratic breathing. Walking down the narrow passageway, she eyed the purple-painted walls that were lit occasionally by triangles of hazy light. The beat of a bass guitar sounded through the walls and the floor. The atmosphere grew heavier as she reached the door at the end of the passage, resonant with a heady mix of heat, sound, and scent. Her heart rate quickened. She paused, noticing that the paint was cracked in the top left-hand corner of the heavy black door, lifting and peeling away, revealing the bare wood beneath. Jade had a keen eye for such things. That was why she had come to The Cave that night, to relish the surface coverings as well as that which lay beneath.

She glanced down at her outfit, hoping it would blend in with what she might find beyond the door. A cut-off latex top, sleeveless and skin-tight, left her midriff bare. A leather miniskirt was cinched around her hips, zippered from waist to hem at both front and back. Shiny soft plastic boots clung to her legs, like skins on her own skin. The decadent outfit gave her cover; it also gave her nerve. She lifted her chin. Jade was a shy but deep-down determined sort. She had an insatiable curiosity for all things sexual, which was inevitably leading her on, and she could insinuate herself into most places with utter stealth.

The door opened and a figure darted past her. Jade took a deep breath at the scene beyond. The room was full of bodies, moving, dancing, whispering against one another. The sound was vibrant, industrial dance music that sliced through the senses. It invaded her body with its powerful, undulating rhythms. A pulse point rapidly began to pound inside her. Flashes of brilliant color broke the pools of darkness that met her eyes: a transparent neon shirt flickering with movement, a streak of deep-scarlet satin hanging low on a tattooed back, white skin shining beneath the black straps buckled across a dancer's back.

Strobe lights sprang to life, flashing a series of frozen images of the crowd in negative versions of themselves, before submerging them again into a heaving, dark mass of dancing. Fetish. Alternative. Jade smiled. How could she not love a fashion that revealed the body with such erotic candor? A wave of heat was building between her thighs.

She slipped easily among the bodies, unseen, brushing against them, her eyes taking in each and every clinging fabric, wistfully peeling them away in her mind. There was nothing like luxurious, fetishistic fabrics to reveal the erotic potential of the body beneath. After seeing a TV feature on the London fetish and alternative scene, Jade had abandoned the mainstream clubs she used to go to with her girlfriends or the gang from the office. She was working her way through a list of London alt.clubs with a mixture of arousal and trepidation. Had she known how tempting an eager innocent was to the fetish generation, her arousal might have reached boiling point before she'd even set foot inside one of the venues.

A woman in PVC sidled past her. Jade closed her eyes and breathed appreciatively. Like latex, PVC molded to the skin by virtue of the heat it met. The material outlined the body, emphasizing every naked inch of skin beneath, every curve, every ridge. Peeling warm PVC or latex off after a night constricted in the body-hugging material was one of Jade's more pleasurable indulgences. The way the malleable, synthetic material lifted away from the skin beneath was exquisite. Shocked naked, every square inch of the skin felt the cold air racing over it, every nerve ending felt wired with sensation. It was one of the most delicious sensations she could imagine, and she wrestled with fantasies about sharing it with another, allowing someone else to peel back her synthetic skins and reveal what lay beneath. She had trod this path alone—a tourist silently observing, yet with her imagination running wild.

Jade headed toward the bar, a strip of smooth black onyx dividing the space between two dance floors. She leaned over it and gave her order to the barmaid, a woman with a crown of bleached hair and heavily kohl-lined eyes. The woman was dressed in a white sheath of a top, Lycra. It revealed her nipples, rock hard and aggressive on her lean chest. Jade turned away and drank her wine quickly. Her fingers traced the cool line of the marble bar and her eyes flickered over the scene in front of her. The place had an attitude of open appreciation about it, everyone eyeing each other and preening for the approbation of others. Jade put the empty glass on the bar and began to edge around the crowd. When she came on the ladies toilets, she entered and moved close to the mirror to check her makeup.

The bright light made her look paler than ever, so she reached into her bag for lipstick. Despite her dark hair, her skin and lashes were pale. Another lick of red strengthened her mouth. She unwound a tiny lid liner and began to outline her eyes. Her hands trembled slightly and the line escaped her control.

"Damn," she breathed, and dropped the liner on the shelf in exasperation.

"Here, let me do it for you," a voice behind her suggested. She turned and saw a woman with a shock of black hair standing some five feet away from her. She was watching Jade with a smile on her lips. Jade glanced at the scarlet dress that clung to her statuesque figure and remembered the flash of scarlet on the dance floor. It was heavy satin and pooled in all the right places—between her breasts, into the groin, around the thighs. Jade flushed when she realized the woman was smiling at her, as if aware of her wandering eyes. Was she being too obvious about looking? She glanced away. The woman sidled forward and picked up the lid liner.

"When I was a teenager, I used to do makeup for all my girlfriends. Now, lower your eyelids." Jade complied, and her downcast eyes took in the red toenails that peeped from the toe of the woman's low-slung black suede shoes. The black straps that bound her ankles emphasized the lines of her legs.

"They used to come to me, because I could do this really easily on others, but I could never get it right on myself." Jade felt the smooth, damp line cross her right eye in a quick swoop. "Of course, the intervening years have improved my aim somewhat." She drew a second line. "There you go."

"Thanks," Jade murmured. She looked admiringly at the woman. Her hair was thick and cropped into spiky layers around her face. Her eyes were almost black and heavily fringed, her full, sensual mouth painted in a deep plum color.

"I'm Nadia," she said. Then, with a knowing smile, she added, "You haven't been to The Cave before, have you?"

"Jade," she said, before adding meekly, "no, I haven't."

"I thought not. I'd remember you."

Jade felt her cheeks heat. The woman had something very direct and playful about her. Nadia reached over to Jade's upswept hair and pulled out a few strands to hang free, framing her face. The back of Nadia's finger stroked Jade's cheek. Jade shivered with delight, and Nadia smiled.

"Why don't you come along with me, Jade? I know what lovelies you should talk to and whom you should ignore." Nadia linked her arm through Jade's and before Jade knew what had happened she found herself clinched against the lush, inviting woman, who then led her across the club with real purpose. The arm that held her was warm and silky-smooth. The satin dress moved as if it would slide off at any moment. Jade swallowed hard.

Nadia led her over to the bar and toward two men.

"Look what I just picked up in the ladies'," Nadia said. Their heads turned in unison toward Jade. Jade noted the inference in Nadia's comment. *Had* she been picked up? Well, she supposed she had. She felt herself blush, again, and looked at Nadia to avoid the curious stares of the men.

"This is Jade. Jade, meet my fellow creatures of the night. The bleach baby is Carl, the other is Sam." Jade forced herself to follow Nadia's arm as it languidly gestured toward the two men. Carl had long hair, bleached almost white. He wore tight black jeans and a flowing shirt that was tantalizingly unbuttoned, revealing the lean muscles of his chest and abdomen. He was incredibly handsome, with a sexual ambiguity that was fascinating. He smiled warmly, as if her joining them was the most natural thing in the world.

Sam was darker in coloring, with short, spiky black hair. Confidence emanated from him, both in the way he held himself and in the way he looked at Jade, his eyes raking her over with blatant speculation. He was more overtly masculine than Carl and his body was draped over the bar in a manner that seemed to invite a sexual response from Jade. She smiled nervously. His chest looked broad and strong beneath the black T-shirt he had on. Her heart missed a beat—he was wearing PVC trousers. She tried to drag her eyes away from the impressive ridge outlined beneath the fly.

"What a find," he murmured. His eyes continued to rove over Jade's body, taking in the line of her breasts beneath the tight latex top and the inviting zip up the middle of her short leather skirt.

Nadia noticed the exchange, chuckled, and said, "Come on, let's dance."

Jade took a deep breath and willed herself to follow. This was it; this was what she had secretly both feared and desired: she'd been picked up by a bunch of people who looked like their clothes were about to fall off at any moment.

They pressed into the crowd to find a space. The movements of the other dancers transmuted into Jade's body, starting her own responses to the music. The foursome found a small space and made it larger with their bodies. Nadia danced like a stealthy cat, often closing her eyes to trace the music more precisely with her body, following where it led. Jade could feel the beats spread up through the floor and pound right inside her, in that inner flesh that was so sensitive to stimulation of a sensual nature.

When a synthesized thread of sounds sprang up, Jade felt Nadia's hands brush against her body like gossamer strands, arousing the naked skin at her waistline. Nadia laughed suddenly, her wide mouth full and delighted, then Jade felt arms slide around her from behind and Sam's face appeared over her shoulder. His body was pressed against her back, taut and wiry. He moved his body with hers, swaying to the music. He slid his hands over her hipbones and nuzzled against her neck. Her head fell back when she felt his mouth against the sensitive skin of her throat. Nadia moved forward, her arms trailing out to them. Jade shut her eyes, wanting the sensations to last forever.

"Time to go," Nadia eventually said, and the men responded immediately.

They scooped her up and piled into a taxi bound for Nadia's apartment. Somewhere in the back of her mind Jade wondered why she was going with them. She pushed her momentary doubts away, for the adventure was too tempting to be denied.

Nadia's home consisted of the entire top floor of an old Victorian house, converted into a huge studio. It was a gaunt space with a couple of doorways leading off to one side. Filling one side of the huge floor space were a pile of cushions and rugs focused around a low copper table that held a dish, candles, and a lamp. Nadia went over to the table and lit some floating candles in the dish. She flung herself onto the cushions at the far side of the table, waving Carl closer.

Sam arranged himself on the cushioned floor, and Jade sat down near him. She watched the wavering candlelight cast shadows across his collarbone and creeping patterns around his throat. It was an invitation to touch him. He turned his head suddenly, and caught her gaze with a smile. She smiled nervously, and glanced away.

What on earth was she doing here? she asked herself, but she soon forgot the question when she saw Nadia grab Carl around the neck, pulling his mouth to hers. Jade watched as their black and red clothes, the black and blond hair entwined across the cushions. She felt Sam's hand slide around her waist and looked around as he caught her mouth with his, a slow, lingering kiss arresting her movement. His mouth brushed over hers, then he kissed her deep. She trembled. He inclined her body back on the cushions and crept closer, his tongue teasing into her mouth as it opened to him.

Jade heard the movements of the other two, and laughter. Unable to help herself, she drew her mouth from Sam's and turned to look as the black and red clothes untwined again. Nadia had pinned Carl to the floor, straddling his hips and holding his shoulders down. He struggled up against her body, bucking his hips and lifting her. Nadia was slowly pulling the shirt off him, chuckling all the time. Dear God, she was undressing him in front of them all. Each slow, revealing tug on the shirt aroused Jade more. Confusion nettled her. She flushed with embarrassment, instinctively closing her eyes and turning her face away.

"Don't you want to see?"

Her eyes snapped open.

Sam was smiling down at her, his expression provocative. *Yes,* she thought. *Yes, she did want to see.* She wanted to see them naked, and she wanted them to see her, too. She forced herself to turn back.

Carl was flat on his back, his arms out to the sides. Nadia had pulled the shirt right off him, revealing his lean chest and the sinuous twists of muscles in his arms. Jade was riveted. Nadia lowered her head to his chest and teased his nipples with her tongue. He arched up. Her hands roamed over his body in deliberate, knowing movements.

"What is it that you want?" Nadia asked in a low voice as she leaned over him. Carl bowed his body up to her, his head falling back, his eyes tightly shut. "No. You must tell us all," Nadia said, and gave a thoroughly wicked laugh.

"You," Carl said quietly, his eyes still closed. "I want you, Nadia." She fell forward to kiss his mouth.

Jade wondered whether she should feel as if she was intruding, but didn't. She felt herself to be part of the undressing, part of the arousal.

"Jade," Nadia called in a low voice as she lifted her mouth from Carl's. She turned and looked at Jade with a suggestive smile. "I want you to hold him down for me." With that, Nadia leaned forward and pinned his arms by the wrists above his head. She jerked her head, indicating for Jade to take over.

Jade was spellbound. She rolled away from Sam and crept over on her hands and knees. She took Carl's wrists into her control. His torso was a streak of white against the dark floor, pinned at wrist and hip by the two women. Nadia bent over his naked chest, licking his skin, her hands roving around his body. He moaned, and his arms twisted beneath Jade's grip. Nadia moved down his body, undoing his jeans, hauling them down his legs, laying him bare. His cock bounced up, hard and eager. Nadia's head lowered. He writhed suddenly and Jade held his wrists tighter. His body arched, and then began to stir in response to Nadia's mouth on his cock.

Jade gasped when she felt a sudden movement at her back and realized that Sam was standing behind her. She glanced around at him. He smiled at her and knelt down, squatting with his knees around the outside of hers, enclosing her body with his, his hands caressing her latex-covered breasts as she leaned over the supine man on the floor. She relaxed into the caress, her hips swaying back to nestle against his.

Nadia was now pleasuring Carl with long, slow plunges of her mouth over his dick. Jade had never seen another woman giving head before, and watched, mesmerized. Carl's arms lifted and struggled beneath Jade's hands, his head moving restlessly from side to side as his body went with the rhythm of Nadia's mouth. Nadia suddenly climbed over him, one knee on either side of his hips, hovering above his erect cock. She stretched up, and Jade held her breath and watched as Nadia lifted the heavy red satin, slowly pulling it up over her head. The fabric moved with a heavy swish over her body, lifting like a theater curtain to reveal the delights beneath.

Nadia threw the dress into a pool on the floor and looked down at the man she was conquering. She was entirely naked, her body now adorned only by the tattoos that crept around her shoulder from her back. Her naked body looked glorious in the candlelight, opulent and pale, yet powerful, like a demon sex goddess. Her eyes brightened with lust, her lips parted with anticipation. She took Carl's cock in one hand and began to lower herself onto it. As the juncture of the naked bodies closed together, Jade swore it was a sight she would savor forever.

She felt Sam's hands moving and then his fingers began to peel up her latex top. She groaned her pleasure, her arms lifting to assist. Needles of sensation raced across the warm skin when it was exposed to the air. Her body shivered with delight. He rested his head into the back of her neck, growling at her reaction. She settled back into his lap; she could feel the bulk of his cock between her buttocks, pushing up against her sex. She wanted to feel it, wanted to feel its skin on her own.

When the latex top was gone, he rested his hands around her breasts, molding them. The sensations between his skin and hers were electric. Nadia smiled at them, her eyes running appreciatively over Jade's body. That they were all looking at her added fuel to her fire. Her head went back, her mouth opened, her hips began to move on Sam's. Jade felt desperate to be part of this. She was watching Nadia fucking Carl; she was moving her hips in time with Nadia's.

"Take your shirt off," she whispered to Sam.

"Gladly."

She cried out when she felt the skin of his chest against her back.

"For fuck's sake, woman, that zipper's driving me wild."

Jade chuckled, the tension mercifully breaking for a moment, and leaned forward so that he could unzip her skirt, splitting it open to reveal her buttocks, bare but for the strip of G-string she wore. She heard his murmurs of pleasure as he unzipped himself, freeing his cock. Her heart began to race again. With one finger he pushed the G-string aside and touched her slit, drawing a line of delicious torture from front to back. He weighted her clit between two fingers, massaging it quickly from beneath. She was bent forward, right over Carl's face, her breasts hanging down toward him. He watched the show with glazed eyes, one woman fucking him frantically, another naked and whimpering with pleasure above him.

Sam began to edge his cock inside Jade. He was hard and felt very big. He nudged his way into her, easing her open to take his girth. She whimpered as he filled her, then physical need took over and she pressed right down onto its glorious bulk. The contrast between his warm skin and the cool, sticky PVC covering his thighs was too divine. His hands guided her hips and she began to ride him with abandon, the feeling of his chest against her back and the sticky pull of the PVC on her bare legs adding their own frissons of pleasure throughout her body.

Nadia was moving frantically on Carl, her fingers clawing at him. Jade could see that they were both about to come. She fell forward again, onto his mouth, plunging her tongue into it and kissing him deep. She gasped when the movement forced Sam's cock up against the front wall of her sex, hitting the spot with uncanny accuracy. The tension in her cunt was building. He began to rut her hard from behind. With each stroke, she plunged her tongue deeper against Carl's. He bucked and came and as he did so his mouth reached up to Jade, meeting her kiss and holding her. Sam pulled at her hips, his cock wedging in tight. She cried out against Carl's mouth when she began to spasm inside, her sex clenching. Sam hauled her body back up against him, his cock deep and hard against her while she came. Her whole body shuddered and he swore low and long, his cock pumping inside her sticky sheath.

She wilted gratefully into the embrace of his arms. Nadia had climbed across Carl's chest with a line of luscious kisses. Jade watched as they kissed, her body still rocking against Sam's. She glanced back. His mouth too inviting, she turned her body and leaned into it again. His hands moved lightly over her body, making her reach for his touch.

"Do you want to come home with me?" he asked. "I live just downstairs." He kissed her again, deeply. He was extremely attractive and his kisses held the promise of more, unhurried passion. She looked down at his half-undressed body. It demanded further attention. She took another deep breath.

Jade was more than ready to help him shed the rest of his night skins.

RACHEL KRAMER BUSSEL

DOROTHY FOR THE DAY

OLLING MYSELF UP to become Dorothy takes a lot of work. First, I take a long, hot shower, then get out and bask in the warmth of the heat lamps. I want my body to be perfectly clean, smooth, and ready for what I'm about to slip it into. After I dry off, I dust myself with cinnamon-scented glittery body powder, watching it shimmer against my legs and wink against my breasts. I shudder as I think of Mark licking his way up and down my body, savoring the spicy flavor of the edible powder, then my own even-spicier taste.

I look over at my blaring red outfit, signaling that I'm a fox on the prowl. Truth is, I could wear a bathrobe or ripped jeans or a poncho, and Mark would want to fuck me six ways to Sunday. But I like dressing up for him, making his eyes almost roll back in his head, making his cock harden at the very first glimpse, making his fists clench with his desire to touch me. I bought the outfit with him in mind, only he doesn't know it yet. It's our anniversary—one year of marriage after ten years of dating—and instead of having a fancy dinner, we're going slumming to our favorite dive bar on the Lower East Side, where fashion is most likely to consist of shaggy and baggy, deliberately expensive tatters, rather than sleek curves and almost-bared breasts and look-at-me legs. I don't care, though—it's where we met, where we belong.

But I have a little trick up my sleeve—or rather, up my panties, since my frilly red dress, light and airy, with its plunging neckline and ruffled hem, so sheer that any breeze threatens to make it fly up, leaves no room for sleeves of any kind. The next weapon in my ensemble is my beloved thigh-high, red patent-leather boots, the ones that simply scream *SEX*. I want Mark to lick them all the way from my dirty soles on up, to streak the shiny material with his saliva. I want him to lick me all over, to make love to me with his tongue—before doing the same with his cock. I love playing games with him, teasing him with my outfits, flashing him when I'm sure someone else will see me. He loves all my games, too, even though he prefers to act embarrassed, but his hard-ons don't lie. Tonight, though, I'm taking things a step farther, I think, as I adjust the shoes. One might call them "Dorothy shoes," as in *The Wizard of Oz,* but only if they didn't have the "fuck-me-now" element to them. I prefer to think of them as "dirty Dorothy," as they channel a sluttier version of our favorite wayward Kansas girl—one who, instead of clicking her heels together three times to come home, spreads her legs as wide as she can and invites everyone she meets to partake of her luscious pussy.

There's only one man I want, but I'm going to make him wait to have me, even though, truth be told, I'd fuck him right now, in or out of my attire. I glance at the clock and see that I'd better get moving if I want to make my proper entrance. I carefully put on my makeup, layering my eyes with thick black liner, then dusting them with silver powder that sparkles, catching the light from all directions. Fake eyelashes complete the look. I open my mouth like I'm about to suck Mark's cock, the thought sending shivers through my body, as I paint on a coating of a solid, stay-on red lipstick, the kind that will get anyone's attention who hasn't already been mesmerized by the rest of my outfit.

Then it's time for the pièce de résistance—a black, bobbed wig, the complete opposite of my long, curly blonde hair. I know Mark will barely be able to resist the stunning, sleek, black-and-red bombshell about to invade his space. I smile wickedly at myself in the mirror, knowing that my beloved husband will find himself with a moral dilemma of the highest order on his hands as this lady of the night tries to seduce him right there at the bar.

I give myself one last stare, seeing a sultry, sexy babe, the kind for whom the word "man-eater" was made. I stalk out the door—that's the only real word for it when your shoes are this high. Thankfully, a cab is waiting right outside my door to take me down from Hell's Kitchen to another, better kind of hell. I see the driver clock me—he probably has me pegged for a working girl—so I spread my legs just enough not to dissuade him one bit. I strum my red-painted nails against my thigh and resist licking my already shiny lips as my pussy throbs against the thin strip of red fabric keeping it from pressing directly onto the seat's plastic. When we get there, I make sure to tip generously and give the driver a little wink as I sashay out the door, tiny beaded red purse swinging from my arm.

Looking like a filthy slut makes the city seem different—more raw, grimy, and fierce. It's not just my added height, it's a new understanding of my surroundings. I'd never wear these kinds of clothes on my own, but knowing that I'm going to meet the love of my life makes me able to revel in their hotness. I look down at my boots, which absorb every ray of light from the street lamps and the cars, and I feel the breeze ruffle my hem as the weight of the wig sinks against my head. I purse my bright lips and smile at anyone—man or woman—who catches my eye as I make my way across the street. When I open the door, even this most jaded of crowds stops and stares. Mark's jaw drops, then he quickly swivels back to the bar, signaling for another drink.

I take a slow gaze around, my eyes making sure each man notices me—and wants me. Then I deliberately sidle up to my befuddled husband, who looks confused. Just as I'd known would happen, he fails to recognize me at all. "Hey, sugar, what's your name?" I ask, throwing some extra honeyed drawl into my words as I lightly run my fingers under his chin. "I'm Dorothy—like in *The Wizard of Oz,* but not so innocent," I finish, smoothly switching my legs so my right touches the air right next to his denim jeans.

"Mark," he manages to choke out, shifting and squirming. "But I'm a married man," he says, holding out his hand, making sure I catch the glint of gold before me. "Just so you know." His words are low, his face flushed and heated.

"Are you, now?" I say, picking up his hand to further inspect his ring, while letting the pad of my thumb press into his palm. He shivers, staring at me before taking a long sip of his beer.

"Yes, I am, and quite happily, thank you very much. I'm waiting for my wife," he says, even as his eyes drink me in, from the stark black bangs of my wig on down to my cherry-red lips, décolleté letting the tops of my breasts merely hint at what's beneath, to my thin, firm thighs, bared between the lacy edge of my dress and the sleek, tight top of my boots. I'd thought about going full-out with the latex, but decided that might be overkill. I like to mix it up as best I can, to throw off guard anyone who's watching too closely. Mark is so overwhelmed by my bulging breasts, bared thigh, attention-seeking (and -getting) boots, and audacious stare that he keeps looking at me and then looking away. When I lean forward and put my hand on his thigh, it takes him longer than it had before to push it away.

I move slowly, like a cat, stretching and clawing, staking my territory ever-so-slowly, not caring whether the rest of the bar is watching or not. Once my entrance has faded a bit, the crowd seems to go back to their beer and gossip and I can enjoy the deliciously hip irony: that nobody would want to be that interested in what I have to offer for too long, and lose points in the art of detachment. It doesn't matter, anyway, because my eyes are only on Mark, who's been my lover now for a third of my life but still manages to surprise me with his boyish charm. His eyes widen, the more I put my energy into seducing him. He's probably wondering why someone like me has immediately decided to pounce on the middle-aged guy wearing faded black jeans and an even more faded heavy metal T-shirt, the band's name eroded after so many years. I run the tip of my shiny boot against his scuffed, worn one, waiting for him to figure it out, giving him time to notice that "Dorothy" is a dream, a mirage, a fantasy—and one that can actually come true.

"So, lover boy, come here often?" I ask, making my voice smooth and sultry, a touch huskier than normal. I know if I laugh I'll give it away, and I'm having too much fun in my new outfit and role to do so just yet. I've worn the dress before, and it's amazing how demure it can look with a proper pair of heels, pearls, and my hair pinned back—why, I could even be someone's mom, a perfect PTA specimen, or attending a fancy brunch at Tavern on the Green with his family, which I've done. Without the wig, lipstick, and boots, it's really a simple dress, but with all the rest, I'm more of a hooker, give or take the heart of gold. I smile my big smile at him, then run my tongue lightly over my smooth, even teeth, the same ones he's been looking at for over a decade. I take a step forward, so I'm off the stool and between his legs, close enough to feel his erection.

I start gently shaking my hips to the honky-tonk song I can almost make out in the back room, and he reaches for my arm to push me back. "Uh, ma'am," he stammers, his supposed Southern gentility warring with the swelling cock I can see and feel so near me. "This just isn't right, I'm sorry. If circumstances were different, believe me, I'd be whisking you out of here right now," he says before it's *his* turn to lick his lips.

It's been fun, but even Dorothy got to go home eventually. I lean forward and gently suck on his earlobe, then let my tongue take a guided tour along that tender cartilage and then inside, not caring about how red I might be making his ear—or his cheeks. "Oh, Mark," I purr, "I think I like our circumstances exactly the way they are."

He pushes me back and stares again, this time with a combination of laughter, amazement, and a hint of awed admiration. "Emily?" he asks, then turns my shoulders around to see if the birthmark on my back is still there, up near my right shoulder, the one that almost looks like a heart if you squint at it. His fingers trace it, and I feel all the love and warmth he puts into that simple touch. His hands go to my hips, then lower, skimming my upper thighs. I know he wants to see if the tiny arrow is still on my ass, the one he dared me to get, the one that only he knows about. I push those hips back against him, so I can feel his cock for real—well, as real as I can between the layers. It's still there, still hard, still just for me. I rub against him for a moment as he reacquaints himself with my body, pulling my head back against his shoulder.

For a moment, I miss my long hair, miss the way it would have tumbled down his frame, spilling over as if it belonged there as my neck arches up, my eyes and lips raised toward the concert poster–plastered ceiling. Then, just like that, I rip off the wig and do let my own natural blonde curls shake loose, down his back, tossing some to the side so they strike his face. After a few more intimacies between my ass and his hardness, I spin forward and give him another blazing smile. "Recognize me now?" I ask, and then, before he has a chance to answer, I give my husband a deep kiss, my tongue slithering into his mouth, overtaking him as I hold him close. I stay there until I need a breath, then pull back, gasping for air, my panties totally soaked.

"'Dorothy,' huh?" he says, coiling one of my tresses between his fingers. "I feel like such a fool for not recognizing you."

"Don't, baby—I would've felt like a failure if you did. I wanted to see if I could still surprise you, if I could still make you catch your

— 25 —

breath and want me like you used to." At that, he grabs me, pulling me close for a deep, intense hug.

"Em, I want you even more now, whether you look like a trashy, but sexy, whore, or whether you're fresh out of the bathtub. You know that. And I would've figured it out eventually, you know."

"I know. But now let's go home and finish what we just started." I saunter out ahead of him, trying to ignore the stares that are directed our way again, now that we're leaving. I'm not sure, but I think Mark might've gotten some very enthusiastic thumbs up from some of the other patrons, and I may have even heard a high five. I'm too busy clicking my way onto the street, thinking about just how I want to come—with Mark's tongue inside me, then with his cock, then…who knows? The one thing I've learned after all these years with him is that anything can happen, and no matter what I call him, or myself, we're soul mates through and through.

Just then, his hand is back on my hip. I'm about to step into a cab, but he pulls me close. "A lady of the night like you shouldn't be so quick to get into her bedroom, should she?" he asks. I wink at the driver, putting my hand behind me to feel him even harder than before, as I let him lead me into a shadowy corner, where I face the brick wall, raise my arms, and give my body over to my husband as he gives his to me. After eleven years, he can still make me come in moments, and I muffle my cries as we do it quick and dirty around the corner from where I'd almost tempted him to stray. "I love you," is the last thing each of us says before coming, his hot lava spilling into me as I clutch him, silently spasming as my climax overtakes me, lasting longer than I would have expected, the rippling aftershocks making me grip him even tighter.

I laugh when I realize I've forgotten the wig, after I dropped it on the ground in my haste to show off my natural locks. But it more than served its purpose. If I need another, for a different sexy disguise yet to come, well, I live in New York City—I know where to find one. I nuzzle against Mark until the air gets too chilly, and then collapse in his arms during our cab ride home.

Happy Anniversary, indeed.

THOMAS S. ROCHE

FRENCH CUT

"DON'T WEAR LINGERIE," YOU SAID when I saw you undressing for the first time. "It's not that I have anything against frilly underthings. It's just not something I do."

I nodded, wanting you naked. Not caring that your underwear is practical stuff: all-cotton jockeys, sports bras, the occasional pair of boxers. Since that initial night together, I've come to understand that you weren't exaggerating. I've *never* seen lace gracing that beautiful, slim body of yours, never seen a Wonderbra caressing those firm breasts or a French-cut pair of panties on your pussy when we undressed for the evening or to make love. You show a distrust of anything girlie, really, but clothing is where your sexy androgyny shows itself the most. You sleep in my old, threadbare tie-dye T-shirts, long enough to reach mid-thigh on your slight frame, and I'm not even sure you know the meaning of the word *stockings*.

It all makes sense, really. You're a natural girl. No meat, just tofu, legumes, the rare slab of salmon. No alcohol, just a few puffs off a joint when you're in the midst of your once-yearly party phase. No coffee, just herbal tea with, now and then, a dollop of honey when you're feeling really naughty. No chocolate, just a sprinkling of carob chips mingling with nuts and berries in handfuls of savored trail mix. For you to wear lingerie would be as strange as a French whore downing a jug of Odwalla and a handful of chlorophyll and superfood tablets.

Which is why it grabs me when I see the lacy white thong riding up above the waist of your hiking shorts. I can't take my eyes off it as I hurry to keep up with you on the difficult trail. For the first few minutes, I want to tell you, want to sneak up behind you and whisper in your ear that I've noticed. But I remember your lecture, when we started hiking together, about wearing sensible underwear and cinching your belt tight enough that it doesn't slip down over your hips. I know there's a reason you've broken your own cardinal rules, and something tells me I'm going to find out.

We're close to the summit now, the isolated spot you've told me about where we can see the whole Golden Gate spread out below us like an Impressionist tableau. I follow behind you, my cock tingling in my pants, hinting at a hard-on that wants so badly to spring out into the open air as my eyes linger on the French lace of your thong.

It happens, finally, when you stop and bend over to pick up a pinecone.

"Look," you say. "It's perfect." You've got a natural appreciation for pinecones—they're the seeds of the evergreen, though normally the reproductive potency of this one wouldn't have such an effect on me.

Now, though, it causes my cock to grow hard in my shorts, so quickly and painfully that I have to shift legs and tug at my jockeys.

Because, when you lean forward, I can see down your top—and can see the hint of lace deep in your cleavage, the low-cut bra embracing your gorgeous breasts.

"Uncomfortable?" you ask, smiling, looking up at me, still bent over, cradling the phallic pinecone suggestively.

"Not at all," I say.

"Too bad," you tell me. You toss the pinecone off the trail and launch into a tawdry sprint, your hips swaying more than a hiking instructor would like.

Breathing hard already, I jog after you.

We reach the rocks sheened with sweat, your tank top so damp that when you slip off your backpack I can see the straps of the bra, tempting me even more. I follow you up the last bit of the trail, out onto the plateau of rocks and dirt sparsely covered with scrub.

"Isn't it gorgeous?" you ask, sweeping your hand over the breathtaking view of the bridge, the ocean, and the bay. You bend over and start rummaging through your backpack; the thong climbs high, your hiking shorts falling further so I can see the curve of your ass.

"Gorgeous," I say.

You take out the blanket and spread it on the dry brown grass. You take out two plastic wine glasses, set the small insulated lunchbox on the edge of the blanket, and stretch out beautifully in the slanted morning sunlight.

"It's awfully hot," you sigh. "Don't you think it's hot?"

"Sizzling," I say as I come toward you.

"Only one way to cool down," you tell me, and reach for the buckle of your belt.

I stop in my tracks, watching as you unfasten your belt and slide your shorts down your smooth, tanned legs. The skimpy thong you're wearing plunges so low I can see the top of your blonde hair, and there on the front of it, rimmed by lace, is a little pink heart.

You kick off your running shoes, slide off your socks, and reach down to pull up the sweat-soaked tank top. When you pull it over your head, I see that the bra matches the thong, a girlie push-up that makes your slight breasts look two cup sizes larger. The cups are so low-cut that they almost reach your nipples, which have gotten quite hard and are sticking plainly through the transparent sprinkling of lace. On the cups themselves is a pair of pink hearts, flawlessly matching the one on your pussy.

"I just love to undress out in nature," you tell me, smiling as you see my eyes drinking in your lace-clad body. "Don't you?"

I take the hint, dropping my backpack and stripping off my sweaty T-shirt, then kicking off my shoes and pulling down my hiking shorts and underwear as one. Your eyes linger over my erect cock, pointing toward you and slightly inclined like a come-hither finger begging you to come to me.

But I'm the one coming to you, I know. You lie down on the blanket, stretching deliciously out and turning from side to side so I can see both the infinitesimal string slid between your buttocks and the tiny patch of heart-adorned lace that covers your pussy. You smile flirtatiously.

"I went shopping yesterday while you were napping," you say. "I don't know what came over me."

I join you on the blanket, pressing my lips to yours and feeling your tongue surge into my mouth. My hand finds your nipples, feeling them harden still more under my touch, and the feel of them poking through the girlish lace excites me even more than I expect. Your fingers curve around my hard cock and you smile when our lips part.

"I'm hungry," you whisper. "Are you hungry?"

"Starving," I growl.

"Good," you tell me, and roll over, away from me. I reach out to touch your ass, fascinated by the unfamiliar way the lace thong looks against your tan.

You unzip the lunchbox and take out a small plastic baggie, frosted with condensation. You roll against me, pushing me onto my back and climbing atop me.

"Say 'aaaaaah,' " you tell me. "And close your eyes."

I do it, opening my mouth. The cold morsel I feel between my teeth shocks me. When I bite, I taste the mingling of forbidden dark chocolate with the taste of strawberries.

"Oh, wow," I mumble, my mouth full.

"Shhhhh," you say. "Just taste. Keep your eyes closed."

I savor the taste of it, ripe and rich and invigorating. I hear you chewing, and when you kiss me, your lips taste of chocolate and strawberry. "Keep them closed!" you laugh.

I feel you shifting on top of me, reaching out to the lunchbox. You place a chilled orb in my mouth and when I bite down I feel the sugared juice of a cherry overwhelming me. You kiss me, hard, your tongue slipping in and lapping at the syrupy confection.

"One last time," you say. "Sit up a little. Keep your eyes closed."

I hear the twist of a screw-top, the faint *glug* of liquid. You place the rim of the plastic glass in my mouth and your hand on the back of my head, telling me when to tip. Red wine floods my mouth, and I feel it dribble warm onto my chest even as I recognize the aromatic flavor—merlot.

"Messy, messy," you say, bending down to lick the droplets of wine off my chest. Your tongue remains against my skin as you lick up to my throat, then kiss me, your mouth tasting of sweet chocolate, fruit, and wine. You take a drink yourself and curl up on top of me, the soft lace of your bra caressing my face as it darkens from the droplets of red wine still slicking my lips.

"I would have brought a cigar," you tell me. "But that would have been going too far."

I'm overwhelmed. I have to have you. My mouth finds your nipple through the lace and I bite gently, suckling it into my mouth. You gasp softly as my tongue deftly pushes the lace down so I can get to the smoothness of your erect bud. Then you're moaning, as my hands cup your ass and gently tug the lacy crotch of your thong out of the way.

"If I'd known chocolate and wine would have this kind of effect on you," you sigh as I guide you onto my cock, "I would have done this months ago."

Then you're not speaking, you're moaning, as I feel the head of my cock parting your lips, feel you sliding down onto me, hungry with need, my shaft filling your cunt as my mouth teases your nipple. The lace against my cheeks feels strange, erotic—but that's not the reason I

— 34 —

want you, nor is it the chocolate or the wine that's intoxicated me. It's the feel of your cunt around my shaft, the desperation with which you slide my cock deep into you.

When I grasp your buttocks and roll you over onto your back, the wine goes flying and spreads a dark stain across the blanket. Neither of us pauses, even as the bottle tips and a stream of merlot begins to pool under you. I slide into you deeper, your legs going easily up onto my shoulders as I pick up the bottle and empty it over your breasts.

"My new bra!" you breathe, only able to speak in mock despair for the faintest instant before my cock reaches its deepest point inside you and you thrust up against me, your lips open wide. I lick scarlet wine from your breasts as you clutch me tight, your hands running through my hair, your body meeting mine with each hungry thrust. By the time you're ready to come, I've reached out and snatched another chocolate from the baggie.

"Open your mouth and say 'aah,' " I tell you, and my thumb teases open your lips just far enough to slip the treasured chocolate cream onto your tongue. You take the whole thing in one bite, your eyes closed, savoring the sensations. I'll never know if you actually come at the very moment you taste the chocolate, because you're one of those girls who comes so hard and so long that isolating your moment of pleasure is next to impossible. But the twist of your body and the arch of your back tells me that it's close enough for lovers. I fuck you harder as you chew the cream and swallow, your moan rich and thick around the textured confection.

Then I shut my eyes tight, on the brink of orgasm, and I should expect it—but I don't.

Somehow, without missing a beat, without lessening your own pleasure, you've managed to reach out and snatch a lemon crème from the baggie, even as it opens and the chocolates scatter across your belly. Your fingers pop the crème into my mouth and its taste fills me at the instant I come, orgasm and sweetness blending in a flash as I thrust deep into you, feeling myself clench far inside your body. When I sense your legs descending from my shoulders, your thighs caressing my sides, I settle on top of you and feel the squish of chocolates between us, coating your skin and mine in the melted ooze of indulgence.

I lick the chocolate from your breasts, feeling only a tinge of sadness as I look at your ruined bra. You unhook it and squirm out of the bra, then reach down and slide off the thong, looking distastefully at it as I see that the chocolates and wine have run down, staining the pink heart with our jealously guarded vices.

You toss the lingerie into the brush, leaving them for some lucky hiker to puzzle over. You smile up at me, your face and breasts moist with wine and melted chocolate, looking even more lascivious, somehow, than the skimpy lace did.

"See?" you sigh. "I never should have let that lingerie salesgirl talk me into this. What have I been telling you? Chocolate and wine are filthy habits." You snuggle up closer to me, our skins sliding together with the mixture of drink and debauchery.

And when I kiss you, I taste them both. Sweet, like you, and just as forbidden.

MaRK WILLIamS

DOMINATED DOLLY

D OMINATED DOLLY. That's what I was. Although I swear I never had the desire to wear women's clothing until I met Mindy.

I was a man's man. Straight as an arrow. Not necessarily macho, but certainly a regular guy. Tall, fairly muscular. Not the easiest physique to explore transvestism, I suppose. But Mindy changed all that. Maybe it's her fault I'm the way I am…or perhaps she simply unlocked a part of me I had kept hidden too long.

I met her at the upscale department store makeup counter where she worked, and sparks flew instantaneously. I was ostensibly shopping for perfume for a woman I no longer cared about, and she sensed my plight immediately. We laughed effortlessly at each other's jokes, and I was mesmerized by her energetic magnetism. Bright-red hair. Mint-green eyes. Small breasts, shapely legs, and what appeared to be a perfect ass. A strong personality—assertive, aggressive, almost domineering.

She encouraged me to stick around until her shift ended, promising to help me find the perfect gift for my (soon to be ex-) girlfriend. After she spritzed various scents on her wrists for me to admire, she gently rubbed up against me in her cotton floral sundress, and I was a goner.

She took me home that night and, in the course of foreplay, playfully asked me to wear her panties. Eager to get laid, I obliged, somehow squeezing them over my sizeable thighs. My cock had never felt harder than it did with her undies encasing it. She teased me in a variety of ways for well over an hour, with my cock tucked into her silky prison.

When we finally made love, my orgasm was surprisingly intense. Mindy credited her panties. I couldn't argue.

A few evenings later, after a quiet dinner followed by a short but wild night of dirty dancing at her favorite nightclub, she insisted that I don her thigh-high stockings after she eased them off. I made love to her that night wearing her nylons, and the silky feeling of my covered thighs against her bare body again brought me to one of my more powerful orgasms in memory.

On subsequent occasions, she would blindfold me with her scarves—always silk, and in a variety of colors—and gag me securely with her bras and panties so I could taste the fabric she had just worn, along with her scent. She would brush against my naked flesh with cashmere sweaters, and the sensation would make me hard almost immediately. One night, she wore only a satin slip and insisted that I fuck her repeatedly without removing it. Total ecstasy.

As weeks passed, I was in a constant state of arousal around her, never knowing what she was wearing or might make *me* wear. She was a merciless fabric prick-tease, and I felt powerless around her.

One rainy Sunday afternoon in late fall, I nervously yet eagerly allowed her to handcuff me to her bedframe. She was still fully dressed from her shift at the makeup counter; I was already naked, my hard-on raging. She slipped off her shoes and peeled off her coffee-colored knee-highs. She then pulled one stocking over my throbbing cock, making sure the toe portion fit snuggly over the head of my dick.

The sensation was absolutely maddening. She repeated the process with the second knee-high. I felt as though I were now wearing a nylon condom, yet my arousal built. She sat on my face and I licked her to several orgasms as my cock flopped around like some sort of silky fish. When she finally jerked me off, I soaked her stockings beyond belief.

"Mindy…" I gasped.

"Halloween is coming, Jason," she said sternly, "and I want you to be my bitch."

I didn't understand.

"I want you to dress totally in drag for me. We're going to a Halloween party as sisters…"

The thought terrified yet intrigued me. "If that's what you want, baby."

"That's what I want, and it's what you really want, too, isn't it?"

I couldn't answer.

The evening before Halloween was to be our dress rehearsal. I was instructed to leave my office as early as I could sneak away. Mindy was going to transform me to her total satisfaction. I was powerless to refuse or resist. She informed me that she had, over the course of a few errands, picked up a wardrobe in my approximate size, and I was to become "Jasmine." I was ordered to get naked, and quickly complied.

With a brand-new electric razor, Mindy proceeded to shave virtually all my visible body hair—chest, back, legs, underarms, even pubes. With a bit of help, I donned silky black Lycra panties that fit me better than any pair of hers, then sat silently as she began to fix my face. Blush, eye shadow, lipstick, various pencils—it was all a blur. A manicure and pedicure followed; bright-red nail polish soon covered my perfectly groomed fingernails and toenails. Mindy had put her years of counter experience to flawless use on me, and when she finally let me glance at my reflection, I was stunned at the "woman" I had become. I didn't recognize myself. I actually felt feminine, despite the swollen hard-on hidden (barely) in my undies.

"You almost look hot," she said, giggling.

Next came my wardrobe. A queen-sized pair of navy-blue panty-hose that I put on awkwardly while she watched. A large bra with padding already inserted. She hooked it for me, knowing I'd never be able to reach behind my back for such a maneuver. A silky ice-blue slip that glided sensually over my hairless body. A belted navy knee-length skirt that was just a bit tight at the waist, causing Mindy to playfully taunt me about my weight. A long-sleeved polyester white blouse that made me shiver when I put it on. Navy-blue pumps (size eleven!) to complete my ensemble. She had thought of everything.

One final touch. "Wait here," she commanded. She returned with what appeared to be a hatbox, and produced a fiery red wig that came dangerously close to matching her own hair color. She tugged it force-fully onto my scalp, clipping it in a couple of discreet places. Then she brushed it into a passable hairdo.

"Well, honey, you're just about done. Stand up and walk over to my mirror."

I nearly twisted an ankle in the pumps, walking awkwardly to obey her command. The visage that greeted me in the mirror was hysterical…frightening…funny…yet incredibly erotic, as well. My cock began to soften, to both my dismay and my relief.

"This is who you really are, Jasmine," Mindy said firmly. "This is not just your Halloween costume. This is who you'll be for me, whenever I want you to. We'll have to work on your voice, of course—and that walk has no grace at all—but you will learn."

"I'll do anything for you, Mindy," I replied. My hard-on once again strained against its nylon panty prison.

"Yes, you will. Now go lie down on the bed for me, darling—face down."

I did as told. The silkiness of my panties, hose, and slip made me dizzy and lightheaded. I thought I might faint from the excitement of being totally made over. Something so wrong, so forbidden, yet it felt so completely right with Mindy.

"Lift up your skirt, honey." I did so to the best of my ability, and I felt Mindy firmly pulling down the waistband of my pantyhose, then my panties. As I turned slightly to try to assist her, I saw the strap-on black dildo that sprang like a black rubber panther from her crotch.

My cock, already swollen and throbbing, again sprang to rock-hard status.

I truly was about to become Mindy's bitch and couldn't imagine resisting. As it turned out, I came quickly and explosively, just seconds before she did. And I knew there would be more days and nights of dressing up ahead.

THE MYSTERIOUS AFFAIR AT STYLES

AVID THOUGHT IT WAS LIKE every Agatha Christie novel he'd ever read.

Lazy rain lashed the night-blackened windows. Only candles and the ghost of a fading fire lit the drawing room. The guests (or suspects, as David now thought of them) lounged on settees and convenient chairs. They sipped at cocktail glasses, smoked cigarettes through elegant tortoiseshell holders, and exchanged an idle banter of shallow pleasantries.

David stood before the fire and stared at the five women. "The culprit is one of you ladies," he declared. "And I think I've finally worked out which one it is."

Eyebrows arched.

Speculative glances were tossed in his direction.

Lavinia giggled as she splashed cognac from a decanter into a balloon glass. "Culprit, Davy?" Her voice was slurred from one tipple too many. "Who's been culpritting?"

"Yeah," Sonia agreed. "What are we supposed to have done, David?"

All five women regarded him with polite expectation. A fug of tobacco smoke hung in the air. Staring at them in their costumes for the themed '20s weekend, he thought it was like looking at a nicotine-tinted photograph from days gone by. The combined weight of their cool appraisals made him want to squirm. But he remained stalwart and steadfast.

Mousy, blonde Talia, anxious as always: "What have we done, David?"

"Fess up, Davy." This was Maria, confident to the point of arrogance. In her typically confrontational manner she asked, "What's the charge?"

Only Olivia said nothing.

David wondered whether her silence implied something. Or whether he was merely clutching at straws in his bid to discover the guilty party. Did Olivia say nothing because she feared he might recognize an inflection in her voice? Or was she naturally taciturn? He racked his brains, trying to remember any conversation he'd had with her since the weekend began. As the silence dragged on, and the five women continued to stare at him, he realized he would have to think about the matter later. For now he needed to supply an answer to their question.

"Last night I was accosted," David began gruffly.

It was a fact.

But it was also one hell of an understatement.

The last to leave the drawing room, after turning off the lights and ensuring that the fire was dying he stepped into the darkened hall. A woman's body pressed close to his. Feminine fingers slipped against his cheek and then went to the back of his skull. More fingers slipped to his waist and trailed down to his groin.

The hand at his groin caressed him intimately.

Through the fabric of his trousers, inquisitive fingertips traced the shape of his length. Before he could draw a startled breath, his head was pulled against a pair of soft, yielding lips. A tongue plundered his mouth as the hand at his loins stroked him to hardness. Plump breasts pushed against his chest. The scent of a deliciously floral perfume filled his nostrils. His initial panic subsided and excitement flooded his body. A long, coltish leg rubbed against the outside of his thigh. The kiss lingered for a glorious age. And, beneath the floral scent, he caught the musk of feminine excitement.

His hands reached for her breasts. He found their shape and noted that they were large enough to fill his palms. A thin layer of silk covered them and he caught the sensation of stiff nipples brushing through the gossamer fabric and touching his fingers.

He held her briefly, savoring the kiss, the caress, the contact.

And then she pulled his hair.

"Accosted?"

"What does that mean?"

"Who accosted you, Davy?"

"If he knew who accosted him, Talia, he wouldn't have summoned us here, would he?" Maria glowered at the meek blonde.

Again, Olivia said nothing. She regarded him from behind fluttering eyelashes. Long dark curls framed her pale, elfin face. Like the rest of the guests (or suspects), she was dressed in a fashionable ensemble. Olivia's costume emphasized her full breasts and narrow waist. Her expression was enigmatic, beguiling, and perplexing. She certainly had a build that matched that of the woman he had encountered the previous night. But David knew the same thing could be said for the rest of them.

"What happened, David?" Sonia wasn't always the first to ask questions, but with Lavinia giggling drunkenly he supposed she had become the group's spokeswoman. "Tell us all about it," Sonia encouraged.

He blushed.

The memory was enough to make his temperature soar.

The woman pulled his hair. He was so startled that he immediately released his hold on her breasts. The hand at his groin tightened. Manicured nails pressed into the pulsing heat of his shaft. Separate pains in his scalp and his erection vied for his attention. The contrast between the excitement of the kiss and the agony of those torments was shocking.

"Never touch me without permission," she hissed. "Never!"

He tried to place her voice and couldn't.

He knew each of the women sharing the house for the weekend. But he had never heard any of them hiss with such passion and ferocity. The anger and power in her tone were deafening, even though they were no louder than a sigh.

"You don't touch me, David," she growled. "Not without my permission. Do you understand, you little worm? Is that clear, you worthless maggot?"

As she spat her muted questions, she gripped him tighter. Her hold on his hair was hard enough to drag strands from their follicles. But that was the least-worrisome aspect of the torment. Her grip around his length was an agony. He worried that her fingers were plunging through the fabric of his trousers and burrowing into the soft flesh of his shaft. He fretted that she was tearing him, scarring him, preparing to maim him forever.

Perversely, those fears made his arousal throb with greater intensity.

"Do you understand, Davy?"

"I understand," he gasped.

She released her hold on his head.

The hand around his erection loosened but never moved away.

"That was an improper way for someone to handle a young lady," she said quietly.

Her whispered voice was maddeningly familiar. He knew her. He recognized her. But it was impossible to connect the name or face that belonged to the blackened silhouette holding him and heightening his excitement.

"A very improper way to handle a young lady," she said again. "And I think you should apologize now."

"I'm sorry," he stammered. He kept his voice down to the same apologetic hush where hers resided. Panic and disorientation had convinced him that he didn't want the rest of the household to be disturbed and come downstairs to find him involved with one of the guests. All that mattered was appeasing the unstable woman who had surprised him in the main hall. "I'm so dreadfully sorry."

"I want more than words," she breathed. Her hand moved back to his head and he was pushed to his knees. The polished surface of the hardwood floor resounded with a solid thud. From above he heard her whisper,

"I want a lot more than words." She stepped forward and he caught the game fragrance of her wet sex. *"Come on, Davy. You know that actions speak louder than words."*

"I don't think I need to go into the details," David blustered. "It's enough to say I was accosted by an unknown assailant."

Sonia inquired, "Did they hurt you?"

Sobering up quickly, Lavinia asked, "Did they take anything?"

"Who was it?" Talia asked.

Maria rolled her eyes and glared at the blonde. "Which part of 'unknown' confused you? He just said he was accosted by an *unknown* assailant. That means he doesn't know who it was." She glanced at David and said, "What makes you think it was one of us?"

He considered Maria for a moment. She was supremely confident and seemed to take pleasure from cruelly dominating Talia. Wasn't he looking for a woman who was able to dominate others in that manner? Didn't she fit the description perfectly? The woman in the hall had certainly enjoyed dominating, and her propensity for cruelty had known no bounds.

"Don't even think of kissing that until you've had my permission."

He held his breath.

It hadn't crossed his mind to consider doing as she implied. He wasn't even sure what she meant. The hall was dark but his eyes had begun to adjust to the lack of light. He could make out the faint glow of alabaster thighs and the dark bands of stocking tops. As he tried to focus his gaze on the shifting shadows, he puzzled over the dark triangle at the top of the thighs. It was only when he drew another breath that he realized his face was mere inches from the woman's bare pussy. He almost staggered back in shock.

"You may start by kissing my feet."

"What?"

"Don't ask questions, maggot. Just grovel before my feet and put your lips against my toes."

He considered refusing, but the thought lasted no longer than an instant. He didn't know who she was, but he relished the control she had over him. Lowering his mouth to one foot, finding the shape with his fingers then guiding his lips to her stocking-sheathed toes, he kissed it, then the other.

"Good boy," she murmured. "You can be obedient, can't you, Davy?"

"Davy?"

Maria's voice snatched him from his thoughts.

"What makes you think it was one of us?" she asked again.

He shook his head to clear his mind of the constant distractions. "It happened in the hall last night," he explained. "Aside from the six of us, there was no one else here at Styles. Four of you ladies had retired. One of you ambushed me after I'd finished securing the house for the evening."

"Ambushed?" Lavinia was giggling again. "What on earth are you talking about, Davy? You make it sound like a troop of commandos took you down at gunpoint."

David glared at her.

"Yeah," Sonia agreed. "You're not telling us much, David. What actually did happen?"

His cheeks turned crimson.

"You may kiss me higher."

He moved his mouth from her toes to her shins. The silk-covered flesh was salted with her fragrance. The flavor was divine against his lips. Raising

— 49 —

his kisses higher, reaching her knees and then her thighs, he could feel the pulse of his arousal throb with renewed urgency. The scent of her pussy sweetened every breath. Even though he had yet to touch her sex, he felt as though he had drunk every droplet of moisture from within her hole just by breathing.

"Is this getting you excited?"

"Yes."

"Really excited?"

"Christ! Yes!"

"Then I shall permit you to masturbate."

It was a formal way of speaking, and made him immediately discount Sonia and Maria as potential suspects. They spoke in a fashion more prone to profanities and vulgarities. Either of those women would have told him to wank or tug off—not masturbate. As he fumbled for the zip at the front of his trousers, he considered that the woman dominating him might be assuming a role, and therefore curtailing her normal mode of speech. The assumptions and theories tumbled through his mind, reinforcing the knowledge that she could be anyone.

But as soon as the heat of his erection lay across his palm, David was no longer thinking about who she might be, only that she had to be obeyed.

"Masturbate while you kiss my pussy," she insisted. "But you can't ejaculate until I give permission. Do you understand that, maggot?"

David sighed.

David sighed. He drew a deep breath and said, "As I was securing the building last night, one of you ladies surprised me in the main hall."

"I suppose it's better than being startled up the back passage," Lavinia quipped. She chuckled at her own ribald humor.

— 50 —

David glared at her, wondering what she knew about the incident. It was almost as though she was taunting him with her secret knowledge of all that had occurred.

"Tongue it deeper."

Her hand was back on his head. She pulled his hair, guiding him this way and that, forcing his neck back so his tongue could more easily slide into the velvety, wet confines of her sex. His nose was daubed with the residue of her musk, and every breath was colored with her scent. No longer spluttering for air, simply doing as she demanded regardless of whether he was allowed to breathe, David pushed his tongue inside and willed the woman to climax. Her pussy lips kissed his mouth and smothered his nose. The slick flesh drew wetly against him.

His hand no longer rolled back and forth along his penis. Her domination left him weak with the desire to come, and he didn't dare stroke his cock for fear of a premature climax. Whoever she was—and his mind was still trying to find an answer to that particular puzzle—she would be egregiously unhappy if he ejaculated without permission. And, considering that she had already treated him with so much cruelty and disdain, David didn't want to do anything that would incur her greater wrath.

"That's it, you maggot," she growled. Her tone was heavy with arousal. Each word was dragged from her chest on a wave of mounting excitement. She yanked at his scalp as though she had forgotten that her fingers clutched fistfuls of his hair. "That's it, worm. Tongue fuck me deeper: deeper."

He almost came. Her orgasm was so powerful that the radiating waves came close to carrying him with them. She pressed his face hard against her pelvis and bucked her hips forward and into his nose. The sensation of being controlled was so powerful that he had to invest every effort into staving off his climax. He wouldn't allow himself to even think about the spray of musk she spurted into his face.

She was panting as she lowered herself down to his side. In her state of breathlessness he could almost work out which of the guests she was.

"You didn't come, did you?"

"No."

"Are you sure?" she pressed. "Should I taste your cock and see if you're telling the truth?"

She didn't wait for his response. From the darkness he felt silken lips engulf his shaft. A sensuous tongue traced the shape of his glans and then trailed along his length. The frisson of excitement was so strong it was unbearable, but David valiantly refused to let the climax sweep through him. If he came without her permission, she would make him suffer. If he erupted in her mouth, he imagined that her cruelty would reach an unimaginable extreme.

"What an obedient maggot you are," she cooed. "I think you should have a special treat for doing as you're told."

He hadn't noticed that her lips were no longer encircling his cock. The sensation had been so divine that it had continued without the need for her mouth around his dick. He clenched every muscle in his body, hoping the effort would be enough to stanch the inevitable pulse of his orgasm.

"Stay on your knees, Davy," she told him. "But pull your pants down and show me your arsehole. I want to slide a finger inside your back passage."

"Do you know what happened last night, Lavinia?"

"Only what you've told us so far," Lavinia replied cheerfully. "And that's not much, is it Davy?"

He scowled, sure that she knew more than she was letting on, but reluctant to press the point. Before he could decide how best to handle the situation, Maria was calling to him from across the room.

"Lavinia has a point, David. This doesn't concern her, and it certainly doesn't concern me. I'm going for an early night."

He wanted to protest and say that he hadn't finished his interrogation yet. But, as he watched, each of the five women nodded agreement and pulled herself from her seat. He watched them file past him toward the doorway. Maria opened it wide and David caught a brief glimpse of the small area of the main hall where he had suffered his final humiliation.

"How does that feel, Davy? How do you like having two fingers up your ass?"

"Good," he grunted. "Very good."

"Stroke yourself. Don't come. But stroke yourself faster."

He was loathe to obey the instruction. She had forbidden him to climax until she gave permission. If he stroked faster, he knew the orgasm would be torn from his swollen dick. He assumed that there would be a simple solution to the dilemma if she allowed him a moment to think about it. But because her face was close to his, and because she had ingratiated a pair of slender fingers into his anus, it was impossible to channel his thoughts in that direction. Obligingly he rolled his fist up and down his shaft.

"You really do have a tight little ass, Davy. How would like me to wear a strap-on and ride you up there like the little bitch that you are?"

He whimpered. The words were strong enough to push him to the brink of climax. The thought that she might do as she threatened made him struggle to maintain control. He felt sure the orgasm was going to burst from him at any second.

"Do you think I can slip a third finger up there?"

"No." He said it too quickly, too sharply. Worried she might take offense, he said more soothingly, "I don't think I could… I mean…"

"You better be able to take it, Davy," she murmured. "And remember: I won't be happy if you come without my permission."

There was no opportunity for argument. Before David could catch his breath, the muscle of his sphincter was stretched. She had pulled her hand away from his rear—not taking the fingers out but allowing them to linger on the verge of exiting the muscle—and he was almost convulsed by the climactic thrill his body needed. His scrotum was a tight sac that would explode at any second. And his anus was widened to a fresh and unbearable width.

"Stop stroking," she snapped.

He obeyed instantly. His hand moved away from his cock and he simply suffered the indignity of being impaled on her fingers. His hands clawed against the polished wooden floor. Sweat clung to his brow and palpitations racked his body. In the darkness, he saw himself suspended over the precipice of a grand and unending chasm of orgasm.

"Let me stroke that cock for you," she whispered.

Her soft fingers encircled him.

In contrast to the harsh treatment at his anus, her touch was light and sensuous on his erection as she stroked with a gentle rhythm. At the same time she buried her fingers deeper into his backside. The different extremes she provided—pleasure at his cock, and pain at his anus—propelled him quickly to the point of no return.

"Let me stroke you," she breathed. "But don't you dare come until I've given you permission."

Certain he couldn't obey, David groaned.

And with that sound the first convulsions of his climax were ripped from him. The orgasm was powerful enough to be an agony. His rectum gripped hard around her fingers. His cock shuddered and convulsed with the strength of his explosion. His shaft pulsed repeatedly, spraying globules of semen into the darkness. He heard them spatter against the polished floor. The sensation of release was the euphoria he had expected. But, as awareness came back to him, David understood that he had upset the woman who still held his cock and continued to keep her fingers pushed into his ass.

She withdrew from him with obvious disdain.

His butt was left feeling hollow.

His cock felt sore and spent and almost bruised.

"I'm sorry."

"You disobeyed my instruction."

"I'm so very sorry."

She pulled herself away from him and, although he could see nothing in the darkness, he knew she was towering over him. "Lick it up, Davy," she hissed. "Lick up the mess you've made and then go to bed."

Without any thought of disobedience, David did as asked. He worked blindly in the dark, thrusting his face against the polished wood. The taste was obscene. His movements were hurried and frenzied, for he felt desperate to do as he had been instructed in the hopes that he could appease the glorious, unknown tyrant who had pleasured him so intensely.

Yet, when he had finished, David realized she had left him alone in the hall. If not for the aching in his balls, the punished sensation in his rear, and the phlegmatic remnants in his mouth, she might never have been there. He returned to the main room and retrieved a candle so that he could make sure that his cleaning operation had been complete. Although he was anxious to know who she was, he wanted to make sure that all evidence of their encounter had been removed before he retired for the night.

The room continued to look like something created by Agatha Christie, but now it was after the final act and all the characters had left. Deserted, the room made him feel as though he had failed. He would never know the identity of his mystery assailant, and that meant he would never experience her domination again. Frustration and annoyance made his smile bitter and he went to the brandy decanter and poured a balloon glass half full.

He supposed he hadn't wanted to discover whodunit.

He just wanted to know if they could do it again.

Swallowing quickly as the brandy burnt his throat, he paused and listened. Although he couldn't be sure, he thought he had heard a footstep on the polished floor of the main hall. Draining the remainder of the contents in one swig, he carefully went through the process of extinguishing all the candles and putting out the flames in the fireplace. And as he left the room, for the first time since the evening had begun, David's smile was filled with hope.

PaUL ROUSSEaU

SMOKING IN THE BOYS' ROOM

ON'T SIT DOWN," I SNAPPED. Michelle stood nervously in front of the desk, popping her gum and shifting from side to side. She was dressed for the occasion: short, tight plaid skirt decent by only a couple of inches; white stockings; high-heeled shoes; loose white blouse with just a hint of her white, lacy bra showing where she'd carelessly let a button or two come undone. Her blonde hair was in pigtails and she was wearing heavy eye-liner and lipstick. My twenty-eight-year-old girlfriend was dressed up in the height of Catholic schoolgirl drag, pretending to be the naughty slut she'd always wanted to be, the slut she'd begged me to let her become for an evening—and I planned to comply, eagerly.

I regarded her from behind the big desk, tapping the eighteen-inch ruler on my palm.

"Miss Peabody informs me that you were caught smoking. Is this true?"

"Honest, sir! I wasn't smoking, honest I wasn't!"

I stood up, moving quickly. Michelle took a step back and I snapped, "Stay still!"

I came close to her, bending down so my face was just inches from hers. I grabbed a pigtail and sniffed it. It reeked of smoke—ten points for realism.

"Not only smoking, but lying," I growled.

Michelle exclaimed: "The other girls were smoking, but honest, I wasn't!"

I bent closer to her face, sniffing.

"You weren't smoking? You swear?"

She shook her head quickly.

I put out my hand. "Spit out your gum, Michelle."

Nervously, she leaned over and let her bubblegum fall into my hand.

She looked into my eyes, fear crossing her face as I came close. Suddenly I grabbed the back of her head and pressed my mouth to hers, forcing my tongue between her lips as she whimpered and tried to pull away. I held her fast, probing her mouth with my tongue and tasting the telltale residue of tobacco: sharp, rich, nasty.

I pulled back and stared at her. Michelle's red lipstick was smeared across her mouth. I wiped my lips on one of her blonde pigtails and saw its tip rouge faintly red.

"Your excuses fall apart under investigation, Michelle. I recommend that you start telling the truth." I sat on the edge of the desk and tapped the ruler on my palm.

Michelle blushed fiercely and looked down at the floor in humiliation. Her pigtails hung past her shoulders; just underneath them, the telltale peaks of her nipples had begun to stand out quite plainly under the blouse.

"You know the punishment for smoking, Michelle."

She nodded. "Yes, sir," she said miserably.

"If you'd like, you could encourage me to lessen the punishment a bit. Say, by telling me who gave you the cigarettes?"

She looked up at me, her blue eyes wide and bright. "Sir?"

I took her chin between my thumb and forefinger and held her fast while she tried to look away. "Who gave you the cigarettes, Michelle? You know full well that you can't have bought them—you're not old enough. Now, who gave them to you?"

Michelle stared into my face, putting on a beautiful show of being too scared to talk. I could already feel my cock hardening in my pants, and Michelle's nipples were more evident than ever under the blouse.

"Miss Peabody said you were smoking in the boys' room. Is it one of the boys who gave you the cigarettes? Andy Taylor?"

"I—I—I," she began.

"Your parents already told me in our parent–teacher conference that they cut off your allowance because they caught you drinking. So you couldn't have given Andy money for the cigarettes. What did you give him, Michelle?"

Michelle was a gorgeous actress. She looked on the verge of tears.

"I thought so," I said. "You sucked him with that pert little mouth of yours, didn't you, Michelle? He smeared your lipstick all over that pretty face, didn't he?"

Shifting nervously, Michelle nodded.

"Uh-huh," she said.

"Did he have you service his friends, too, Michelle?"

"Just a few of them," she whimpered pathetically. Her nipples were now even more clearly evident.

"How many?" I asked sternly.

"S…six or eight," she said.

"You're sure? Not more?"

"Well, maybe ten," she whispered.

"Ten boys, all using that mouth of yours, just for a few cigarettes. Tsk-tsk, Michelle. Don't you know that even whores your age get cash? What have you got to say for yourself?"

"I—I don't know," she said.

"Open your blouse," I told her.

"Sir?"

"I said unbutton your blouse, Michelle. Right now."

Michelle began to fidget with her top button, looking at me for reassurance.

I tapped the ruler on my palm. "Go ahead," I told her.

She unbuttoned her blouse slowly, letting it fall open to reveal the creamy mounds of her breasts imprisoned in their too-tight, too-low-cut bra. Her nipples peeked out quite clearly. Tucked into her cleavage was a cigarette.

"I thought so," I said. "Give it to me."

She took the slightly crushed cigarette out of her cleavage and handed it to me.

"Anywhere else you're hiding the cigarettes your boyfriends gave you, Michelle?"

She shook her head.

"We'll see. Lift your skirt."

"Please," she said, tears forming in her eyes. "Please don't make me…"

"Lift your skirt, Michelle. Right now."

She took hold of her tight skirt and snugged it up over her thighs, revealing the lace tops of her stockings where they hitched to her garters.

"Higher," I said.

She lifted her skirt up over her crotch, revealing smooth-shaved pussy unhindered by panties. Tucked between her thighs, in the top of her stockings, was a pack of Marlboros with matches in the cellophane.

"I thought so. Give them to me."

She took out the pack of cigarettes and handed them to me. I took them and got one out, lighting it while she watched.

I took a drag and blew smoke at her.

"Would you like one?"

She shook her head nervously.

"I'll bet you would, but you're too ashamed to ask for one. Now, Michelle, care to tell me why you're not wearing any panties?"

"He…he doesn't like me to," she said.

"Andy?"

She nodded.

"Does he like you to shave your pussy, too?"

"N…no," she said. "That was my idea."

"I'm sure it was. Do you like the way it feels?"

She nodded.

"You do realize that only strippers and prostitutes shave down there, don't you?"

She shook her head.

"Well, they do. Which are you, Michelle?"

She looked at me dumbly. I blew smoke in her face.

"You're a whore. At least, that's what your clothing tells me."

"Please, sir…I'll try to be good."

I took a drag off the cigarette, walked over to the couch, and sat down.

"Over my lap, Michelle."

She began to pull her skirt down and I said, "Leave your skirt up."

Nervously, she came over to the couch and lay across my lap, her skirt pulled up so that her pretty derrière was exposed.

"Legs spread."

"Sir?"

"Legs *open,* Michelle. I don't want to tell you again."

She parted her thighs. I set the ruler in the small of her back and let my hand trail up her inner thigh. I was still holding the cigarette.

I placed it close to her pussy, so close she could feel the heat, but not close enough to burn her. She squirmed, her belly pressing against my hard cock.

"Can you feel that, Michelle?"

"Uh-huh," she said.

"Does it scare you?"

She nodded.

"I'm going to spank you, Michelle. But the next time I catch you smoking, do you know where I'm going to put out this cigarette, Michelle?"

She shook her head.

I chuckled. "Oh, I think you know."

I dropped the cigarette on the floor and crushed it out with my foot. My hand returned to her thigh and lingered an inch from her pussy.

The first blow shocked her, made her yelp. She squirmed as I hit her sweet spot again, my fingers curving under to give her exactly the right amount of *thud,* an amount I'd calibrated in years of spanking her—though never in a schoolgirl's skirt.

"Say, 'Thank you,' Michelle."

"Th...thank you, sir."

I spanked her again, my hand beating her firm ass in a slow, mounting rhythm. Michelle began to squirm in earnest, writhing and wriggling in my lap with each blow on her butt. I spanked her faster until she was moaning in pain, whimpering with each blow.

"Th...thank you, sir," she said, without being prompted.

I slipped my hand between her legs, touched her there. She gasped as I slid one finger into her. A thin dribble of juice ran onto my hand.

"You're not a virgin," I said.

She shook her head.

"And you're very, very wet," I said.

She didn't nod.

"Was Andy your first?"

Michelle shook her head again.

I slipped two fingers inside her, curving my hand to massage her G-spot. She gasped and then moaned, pushing her ass against me, forcing her pussy onto my hand.

"You're enjoying this, aren't you?"

— 63 —

Shaking her head, she quickly replied, "No, sir. Please stop."

I worked my fingers in and out of her pussy, making sure that the pads of my fingers hit her G-spot with every thrust. Her wriggling felt incredible on my cock, and I knew I would come before she did if I wasn't careful. When I eased my thumb down to touch her clit, she let out a wild, uncontrolled moan of pleasure and looked up at me with her bright-blue eyes.

"You want it, don't you? Want me to do to you what Andy did?"

"No, sir," she said. "Please…"

"If you don't want it, Michelle, why are you so wet?"

"I…I don't know, sir!"

I started spanking her again—slow at first, then faster and faster as she whimpered and squirmed. I could tell she was very close—she could come from spanking alone if I did it right, but I wasn't about to let my schoolgirl get off that easy.

"Ask for it, Michelle. Ask for it or I'll tell Andy you tattled on him."

"No, sir, please…"

"Then ask for it."

"P…please, sir. Please do it to me…"

"Do what? You know the word, don't you, Michelle? Surely a slut who gives head for cigarettes knows the word for what she wants done to her?"

She said it so softly I almost couldn't hear her: "Fuck."

"Louder."

"Fuck, sir." Louder.

"Ask me for it."

Again, so soft I couldn't hear: "Please fuck me, sir."

— 64 —

"Ask me!"

Louder, almost a groan: "Please fuck me, sir!"

"You want it from me the way you got it from Andy? Then beg for it!"

"I want it, sir! Please fuck me, sir!" She seemed to break through a barrier and whimpered hungrily, "Please, sir! Stick your thing in me, sir! I want it, sir!"

"Show me what you did to his cock before he put it in you! Show me what you did to Andy and his friends in the boys' room!"

She had definitely broken through the barrier. She was down on her knees in an instant, between my spread legs, groping at my belt and pants. She took my cock out and began sucking it fiercely, leaving lipstick traces down the length of it. Michelle was an expert. I knew I would come soon if I didn't hold back. I fought my orgasm, not wanting to lose it before I fucked my naughty schoolgirl. She lavished her love on my prick, sucking desperately.

I knew it was coming soon—I couldn't hold back any longer. It was hard to pull her off my cock. She was so desperate for it, her breasts heaving under the open blouse as she sought my hard prick.

"Turn around," I told her. "Turn around and put your ass in the air."

She scrambled around, getting on all fours and wriggling her ass back toward me. Her gorgeous ass curved around my cock as I fitted the head between the lips of her shaved sex and pushed it in, hearing her gasp of release.

She came before I did—just. I heard her moaning, felt her spasms as she gripped my cock, as I drove it into her rhythmically, and the contractions inside her milked the orgasm right out of my cock. I came, moaning myself as my cock spent itself in her.

My cock slipped out of her. Michelle remained on her knees, moaning, her ass swaying back and forth as she begged for more.

"You're headed right back to the boys' room, aren't you?" I asked. "You can't wait to get back there."

She looked over her shoulder, and smiled.

RAGS TO RICHES

"DAMN," I SAID, PEERING INTO THE BEDROOM window from the ladder I was on.

Chris stopped painting and looked over from his own ladder. "What do you see?"

"That's quite the crib." I was looking into a huge room with a gigantic canopied bed in the middle. Must be nice, I thought. Until I was fifteen, I shared a tiny bedroom with my younger sister. Then I left home.

I kept painting, working on the trim around the window. The Florida sun was baking hot, but despite my Irish blood I'd gotten used to it, having grown up here. I just had to watch my skin—it still burned easily. No bikini tops for me—I had a T-shirt, shorts, and hat on for this job.

Chris didn't have to worry so much—he was black and didn't burn so easily. Right now his bare chest was glistening with sweat and speckled with white paint. Not that I cared much—girls were more my thing. I looked back into the bedroom.

"What kind of a kid has a room like this?" I asked.

"A seriously foxy one," Chris said. I gave him a look.

"Oh yeah. Isabel Fuentes. A couple years older than us, 'bout twenty-two, I think. Smokin' hot Latina. Her daddy's a lawyer, her momma's a head doctor, and she's an only child. They got some cash."

I whistled. "Yeah, that would help explain the mansion here."

By the end of the day I still hadn't seen a soul at the house. "Where are they?" I asked Chris.

"I heard they're outta town, not that we're supposed to know. Rafael knows the guy who maintains their irrigation system. He said the three of them are chillin' in St. Vincent til Sunday.

"Must be nice," I said, a bit bummed I wasn't going to see this Isabel Fuentes.

The next day Chris had to cut out early. After he left, I moved my ladder back to that bedroom window. The backyard was remarkably private, and the previous day I'd noticed the window wasn't locked. I took a good look for motion sensors, but didn't figure there'd be any in an upstairs bedroom. I hopped inside.

I'm not a thief, but I wanted to be rich for a day. Or at least an afternoon or two. I peeled off my sweaty clothes and took a quick shower in an adjoining bathroom that was bigger than my studio apartment. I knew the cleaning ladies came on Saturday, before the family got back, so I wasn't too worried. Naked, I checked myself out in the full-length mirrors—not too bad. Arms a little red from the sun, but body doing fine. Dark tattoos contrasted with my pale skin. My hair, which was naturally Irish red, I kept cut short and dyed black. It stood up when it was wet, giving me a punkish look.

Normally I went for a grunge/goth mix, but this was my chance to try something a little more upscale. I walked into Isabel's closet, marveling at how many clothes she had. I went over to one of the rows of dresses.

I never wore dresses.

So it was weird that a cocktail dress caught my eye, a white one. I carefully took the dress off the rack and slipped into it. The material clung to my skin—I wondered what it was. The dress was strapless, with a satin tie that went under my breasts. But the best part was the back. I have a great ass, and the dress showed it off, clinging to my cheeks. *Either commando or a thong with this one,* I thought, spinning in front of the mirror. I grabbed some gold pumps from the closet—my feet were a bit narrow for the heels, but otherwise they fit okay. Isabel and I seemed to be about the same size.

Back in front of the mirror, I wondered why I was doing this. I looked so different—what was this little ensemble worth? Probably a month or more of painting. I was spinning around in front of the mirror again when somebody walked into the bedroom.

"Shit!" I yelled, and whoever it was screamed. A young woman stood in the doorway, frozen for a second. She was wearing a nice outfit and had dropped a small travel bag. Isabel.

"Who the hell are you?" she demanded. Her eyes widened more. "And what are you doing in my bedroom? In my dress!"

I held my hands out and babbled. "I'm sorry, you aren't supposed to be here. I'm not stealing anything, I won't come back, don't fire Chris, he doesn't know."

She gave me a blank look. I pointed to the open window. "I've been painting your house. I noticed your bedroom window was open. I—uh, I've never really worn anything like this before, and I guess…"

I shut up, hoping she wouldn't call the cops.

She walked into the bedroom. "I got into a fight with Father and decided to come back early," she said. Chris was right—she was gorgeous.

"I'm really sorry," I said, feeling stupid. "Let me just get my clothes and…"

Isabel straightened up, looking less upset. But the gleam in her eye worried me.

"Take my dress off. Now."

I'm normally a dominant person, but Isabel spoke like a queen. Not like a spoiled rich girl, but like a woman used to getting her way. I started toward the bathroom.

"No. Right here."

I stopped. "I'm not really wearing anything underneath…"

Isabel walked over to the bathroom and grabbed my painting clothes off the counter. "I take it these rags are yours?"

I nodded, feeling embarrassed. Shit—I was painting, not going out for dinner. Why should I feel bad?

She walked back into the bedroom. Her nostrils flared. I watched her closely, still wondering how busted I was. She brought my shirt closer to her face. "They smell like…"

"Like paint and sweat," I said. "I've been painting all day, honest, and it's hot out there."

Isabel nodded. A change was coming over her. I took a step forward and reached for my clothes, but those full lips of hers curled into a half smile and she stepped away.

"Not just yet," she said. She motioned toward the mirror. "So, do you like my dress?"

I wasn't sure what to say. Finally I just nodded.

"Well, fair's fair. I'm going to try on *your* clothes."

"Ummm…" I couldn't finish my sentence because Isabel started stripping. Her body was just as attractive as her face, with creamy brown skin and curves in all the right places. She took off her pretty travel ensemble and paused only briefly in her lacy bra and panties before removing them as well. Just as quickly, she pulled on my sweaty painting shirt and shorts.

I stood frozen by the mirror as she strutted around the room, walking like a guy. She stopped right next to me, her eyes burning bright. "Go ahead," she said. "Look at yourself in the mirror. You really do look lovely in that dress."

I didn't want to turn my back on her, but she grabbed my shoulder and spun me around. My mind raced—*at least she hasn't called the cops,* I thought, but this was getting weirder by the second.

Suddenly her body pressed against me from behind. She was warm and strong, shoving me forward against the big dresser. It didn't help that I was a bit tipsy in her shoes. A hand grabbed my hair, pulling my head back. Her teeth brushed against my ear, making my legs even more wobbly.

"Arch your back," she whispered. She pushed my head forward—I had to steady myself with both hands on the dresser. Isabel kept pressing my head down. I could smell my own sweat on the clothes she was wearing. A thigh pressed firmly into my ass, pushing me forward even more.

"I said *arch*," Isabel hissed, yanking my hair backward while shoving her leg between mine. I stumbled slightly, my legs spreading farther apart. I arched.

"God, what an ass," she said, running her free hand over the tight fabric of the dress. Although the tension on my hair lessened, I kept arching my back—her fingers and the leg jammed against me felt too good. Isabelle pressed tight, her hand coming around to squeeze my breast, her mons grinding against my ass.

The grinding became frantic. She pulled harder on my hair again. Ass up-thrust and body jammed against the dresser, I realized she was using me, that she was going to get off on me, here and now.

I was right. Isabel came, grunting and grinding, squeezing my breast so hard it brought tears to my eyes. Despite the pain, I nearly got off myself, thanks to her leg, which was pressed hard between my cheeks, mashing the clingy dress material into my wet pussy. Isabel finished too quickly though, and abruptly let me go and stepped back.

Sore and horny as hell, I slowly straightened up and turned around. She was lounging on the bed, already smoking a cigarette. Smoking a fucking cigarette!

"Don't say anything," she said, and her eyes meant it. "You shouldn't have been in here. You'll get fired and maybe arrested if people find out."

I stood quietly, wondering where this was going. She got up and peeled off my clothing, shorts first and then the shirt. She really did have a fantastic body, toned and strong, and she moved like a dancer. She tossed the dirty clothes at me. I caught a whiff of a new smell added to the paint and my sweat. It made me even hornier.

"You can keep the dress," Isabel said as she walked to the bedroom door. Still completely naked, she turned. "I'm sure you can see yourself out," she said, nodding toward the open window. "Maybe I'll see you tomorrow," she added before leaving the room.

Chris and I were doing the side of the house the next day when Isabel came out to the backyard wearing a minimalist bikini. She gave us both a nod and stretched out on a beach chair. I'm not sure who was more distracted—me or Chris.

Shortly after he reluctantly left, there came a tapping on my ladder. I looked down.

"Back door's open," she said. "C'mon upstairs."

I finished painting, slid down the ladder, and in record time put the brushes away and closed the paint cans. The staircase was just inside the back patio doors—I headed up.

She held out a thick bath towel when I got to her room.

"Trade you this for your clothes," she said.

I stripped and took a shower. When I came out of the bathroom there were clothes displayed on the bed. Pumps, long stockings, a thong, and a lavender dress. The dress was spectacular.

"Go ahead," Isabel said, from over by the window. "Get dressed." Wearing a university T-shirt and a classy looking pair of capris, she looked like a pretty, young woman home from college.

I walked over to the bed and picked up the thong. It wasn't lacy at all and felt smooth as silk, but thicker.

"Microfiber," she said. "You'll like it."

I let the towel fall to the floor and pulled on the thong. It felt very nice, and left my ass completely bare. Next were the stockings. They matched the dress perfectly and came to just over my knees.

"Don't get too attached to those," Isabel said. "They might get wrecked." I shuddered a bit at the implication, and tried to focus on the dress.

It wasn't difficult. This one was a corset dress, the bottom long and billowy, with a delicate net over the thick lavender fabric and white lace underneath. The top would fit tightly, thanks to rows of pink satin straps on the front, sides, and back. I had never held a piece of clothing that felt so…luxurious. Extravagant. Expensive.

"Lovely, isn't it?" Isabel whispered, closer now. Although I was standing in front of her, wearing just thigh-high stockings and a thong, I noticed she was deliberately not staring, like a man trying to be polite.

I held the dress to my chest. "Will you help?" I asked.

Isabel smiled. "Of course."

Moving behind me, she helped me into the dress and then laced up the top tightly. When she was done, my breasts bulged upward and I could only take shallow breaths. Isabel stepped back, and now she stared.

"Dazzling," she said. "You look like…"

I blushed and walked to the mirror, then gasped. "Like a princess," I said softly.

"Yes," Isabel agreed. "*My* princess."

I stared at myself, moving slightly to change the angle. What would my friends say if they saw me like this? It was so different. I spun, and the dress billowed outward. I turned to every angle I could think of, dazzled.

Isabel interrupted my reverie with a small cough. I turned toward her, wondering how long I'd been looking into the mirror. She was close, and I was not entirely surprised to see she had put on my painting clothes.

"It's the smell," she said. "I'm really turned on by smells." She pulled my shirt up, breathed it in.

"Sweat and paint," I said, an echo of the day before.

She smiled. "I think there's a certain…anticipation there, as well, today. Do you think anticipation has a smell?"

Considering how horny I'd been all day, it wouldn't surprise me at all, but I kept quiet.

She took my hand, kissed it, then spun me around and told me how beautiful I was. When she led me toward the huge bed, I followed as if in a dream. I found myself sitting amid a pile of expensive pillows, feeling naïve, innocent, and excited—all at once.

Standing at the edge of the bed, Isabel peeled off the T-shirt she'd taken from me. She wasn't wearing a bra, and her nipples were very dark. I watched, in awe, as she pulled down the shorts.

Underneath she was wearing smooth cotton boy-shorts, a medium-blue color. They hugged her hips and didn't quite cover the bottom of her ass. I stared.

She moved onto the bed and began kissing me with confidence, pushing me back. Before I knew it I was on my back, her lips on my neck and her hands caressing the skin above my stockings, moving higher and higher up my thighs. In a daze, I opened my legs for her and sighed as she lifted the dress and slid between them.

She took my face in her hands and stared into my eyes, whispering how beautiful I looked, how sexy I was. I melted completely, surrendering, opening my legs even farther. She moved into a high missionary position, her pubic bone pressing against my clit. Kissing me slowly, she began to move her hips.

We both groaned with the sensation. The material of the thong was perfect, allowing her to slide against me with almost no friction. I felt soaked, my lips engorged, my clit burning. She clutched my shoulders and moved faster, her tongue in my ear, her voice whispering.

"Come with me now," she demanded. "Don't wait, I need you now, come with me…" Her voice became guttural and her hips went wild. I clutched her ass, pulled her against me, and came fast and hard, yelling unashamedly throughout. Isabel spasmed against me and then collapsed, both of us gasping for air.

After a while, she slid sideways and propped her head up with her elbow. "I don't know about you, but that's how I wanted my high school prom night to finish," she said.

I sighed. "This was definitely a whole lot better than mine." I looked into her eyes. "But I'll bet we've reversed roles."

She smiled. "I wore that dress."

I nodded. "My date decided she wasn't really a lesbian after all— right after we got home and started making out."

"Ouch. Well, Chad—swear to God, his name was Chad!—thinks he came before he'd stuck himself halfway in."

I smiled. "Sex gets better, doesn't it?"

She didn't answer, but got up onto her knees beside me. "God, you're lovely," she said, looking down.

"I feel like a disheveled princess now," I said. The dress was up around my waist. The corset was still too tight, one of my breasts nearly spilling out the top. And the thong was soaked.

She growled a bit, lifting my leg and sliding one of hers between mine. Kneeling above me, she looked stunning, powerful, dominant. Her nipples grew as I watched.

"Can you loosen the corset," I begged.

She pushed my upper body over sideways, but kept my leg pinned between hers. Although my face was mashed into the bedding, I took a deep, grateful breath as I felt the corset slacken off.

Grabbing my arm, she rolled me back. She yanked down the top of the dress, freeing my breasts, and then began to thumb my nipples. I felt my legs opening again. Pinching now, kneeling over me, our legs scissored together, she began to grind, slowly but powerfully.

"This will be a bit rougher," she said, her voice low and primal. Pinned to the bed below her, I wasn't in a position to argue, even if I'd wanted to. A good prom date should last the night. After all, you want to get the most out of those clothes.

PRESENTING PAULETTE

DRESSED HER UP LIKE A DOLL. That's what he had done.

It wasn't that Paulette didn't like it when Warren bought her things—in fact, she loved it. Warren had good taste, for the most part. The wine glasses he had given her for a housewarming gift—those were nice. That naughty latex lingerie he surprised her with on Valentine's Day: he had practically read her mind.

But this…Paulette just didn't know what Warren was thinking.

She was going to tell him no, to take it back, that she didn't give a damn what his reasons were, he could take it all and shove it up his ass.

But she didn't. She couldn't.

It had nothing to do with manners. Paulette would return a gift quicker than you could blink, but this was different. This came from Warren, who had a way of convincing her of things, of making her see things differently even when her mind was already made up.

Simply put, it was the sex. Nothing else.

The sex, it made her foolish. Warren could fuck her into jumping out of a plane if he wanted. Indeed, he had fucked her into wearing this ridiculous outfit.

It was only a few weeks ago that Warren had come over, bags in hand, goofy grin on his face. He had pulled the top out of the bag first, then kissed her quickly on the neck before she could get a good look at it. He held up the skirt next, then slipped his tongue in her ear while she tried to explain to him that it was just too damned long for her taste.

Now she sat behind the wheel of her Mustang, twitching in her seat because the fuzz from the sweater made her itch. She didn't know what made him think she would look attractive in the thing, anyway. It covered up all the good stuff and made her chest look flat. His mother would like it better, he had told her.

Maybe his mother didn't have breasts.

The hem of the heavy corduroy skirt kept getting caught around the clutch, and Paulette had to hike it up around her thighs to shift gears. The skirt, she had argued, did nothing for her figure. It was so long and heavy that you couldn't tell there was anything underneath, but Warren said his father always complimented women who wore pants and long skirts.

Maybe his father had never seen a pair of legs.

Paulette struggled to downshift when she approached a red light. She was used to driving in heels, but Warren had picked a pair of plain brown flats. He had snuck those in, just like he did the rest of the outfit.

Paulette didn't even wear flats; Warren knew that. She didn't like them and they didn't look good on her.

In fact, none of it looked good on her. Not one piece. The whole outfit was plain, drab.

It was neutral, and Paulette was anything but neutral. Paulette was emerald and purple and cobalt-blue. Neutral was safe. Neutral was boring and predictable.

She shifted into first gear and pulled away when the light turned green. She shook her head. She thought Warren knew her better.

Paulette reached up and patted her hair, glanced at the short, slick pageboy in the rearview mirror. Warren had picked the style out of a magazine. She ran her fingers through it. It wouldn't be long before the little waves began to reappear. Her hair didn't even know how to be straight.

It was only three hours out of her life, Warren had assured her, and that was fine. But what about after today? What about when his parents decided to visit him in New York and she was there? What if they saw that she liked her skirts short, her shirts tight, and her hair wild?

Of course, Paulette knew how men were about their parents. She knew that this was big and she should be appreciative, not sweating over something so simple as an outfit. Hell, Warren had waited until they had dated nearly nine months before he even considered introducing her to them. She, by contrast, had invited him to dinner with her and her mother after only three weeks.

Paulette glanced at the index card with the directions jotted on it and turned down the suburban street. Her yellow Mustang looked out of place in a neighborhood full of luxury cars and expensive SUVs. Still, she guided it into the empty space next to Warren's BMW.

Paulette stepped out of her car. She straightened her skirt and brushed at her sweater. Not that it did her any good. Not that it made the ensemble any less plain.

She reached up and smoothed her hair one final time and knocked.

Warren opened the door. He gave Paulette a once-over and smiled, seemingly relieved. Did he think she was going to change her mind at the last minute, show up in an outfit of her own choosing just to spite him?

His attire was equally plain. He wore chocolate-brown slacks and a pale-yellow shirt. His hair was cut low. He had trimmed his beard and mustache and taken out his earring.

Paulette saw a short, shapely figure approach him from behind.

Warren turned and guided the woman forward so that she stood beside him in the doorway.

"Mom, this is Paulette," he said and gestured with his hands as if he was presenting a prize.

He was absolutely grinning. Looked like a goddamn cheetah.

The woman nodded, extended her hand, and gently shook Paulette's. "It's nice to finally meet you," she said.

Mrs. Vaughn was just as Paulette had imagined her. She stood there, well put together in a soft-pink blouse and pleated gray slacks. Her hair was pulled back into a tight bun. Her makeup was soft and minimal.

Warren's father came down the stairs and stepped slightly in front of his wife. He was tall, had a full-beard and mustache that was peppered with gray. He greeted her with a firm handshake and smile.

Paulette stepped inside and Mrs. Vaughn reached for her coat and hung it on the rack. She wished she could keep it on, keep the sash pulled tightly around her waist so that they wouldn't have to see the hideousness that lay beneath.

Paulette simply nodded when the Vaughns offered her a tour of the house, and as she followed them from room to room, she silently prayed that she wouldn't trip over the train of corduroy that wrapped around her legs.

Paulette wasn't sure why the size of the house surprised her. Warren's parents were well off, she knew that. Still, she felt overwhelmed sitting with them in their grand dining room. She felt out of place, like a pig in a museum or something.

The four of them ate their dinner in silence but for the occasional clinking of ice against glass and fork against plate. Paulette felt she should say something—compliment Mrs. Vaughn on the meal, praise the centerpiece or the china service—but she kept her mouth full and her smile plastered on.

She thought it best if she didn't say much, if she just grinned and chewed silently instead of leaning over and asking Warren how it felt sitting next to a complete stranger at his family's dinner table.

Warren glanced at her now and then, reached over and placed his hand on hers when she was fidgeting. He touched her knee when she was shaking her legs too much.

The first interrogation came from Mrs. Vaughn. "So, Paulette, Warren tells me you work in retail?" She set down her fork and folded her hands on the table.

Paulette glanced at Warren, who avoided her eyes. "Yes, ma'am, I manage a fabric store in the city."

Mrs. Vaughn nodded. "Have you lived in New York all your life, or did you just come here for school?"

Paulette forced the mouthful of salad down. "I grew up in Brooklyn," she said. "I left there when I was seventeen. I started working at the store then."

"So, you didn't attend college?" Mr. Vaughn interjected, leaning forward, his head cocked.

"I'm in school now, taking night courses. I'm working to become a designer." As soon as she said it, Paulette realized that it sounded more like an explanation than a general addition to the conversation.

Warren finally chimed in. "Paulette's quite talented. Almost everything she wears, she makes."

Mrs. Vaughn sat back in her chair, her eyebrows arched. She scanned Paulette's outfit, which made Paulette shift uncomfortably in her seat.

"Warren picked this out, though," Paulette said.

Mrs. Vaughn turned to her husband. "Charles, didn't I used to own something like this?" she asked.

"I believe so," he said, "I believe you had it in lavender, or blue or something."

And it was then, just after the fish course and before the dessert, that Paulette thought she would be sick. The sleeves of the sweater were suddenly tight on her arms. The waist of the skirt was making it hard for her to breathe.

Paulette pushed her chair back and dropped her napkin on the table.

"Excuse me, Mr. Vaughn…Mrs. Vaughn," she said and slipped through the nearest cracked door, hoping that on the other side of it was a toilet.

Relieved, Paulette sat down on the covered lid and looked around. The sherbet-orange color on the bathroom wall was nauseating. She placed her face in her hands and forced herself to breathe. In. Out. In. Out.

It sure was hard work performing for Warren's parents.

Paulette didn't understand. If Warren had wanted prim and proper, someone who would wear an outfit like this, and fit in perfectly with his family, he could have had that. But he had chosen her, had walked into her store that afternoon and taken her just as she was.

Paulette was a lot of things, but one thing was for certain—she wasn't a fake.

She was thinking of going back out and telling his parents she didn't feel well and she would be heading back to the city early, when the bathroom door creaked open and Warren came in.

He pushed the door closed behind him. "I just wanted to come in and check on you, make sure you hadn't climbed out the window or something," he said, smiling.

He shoved his hands in his pockets, rocked back on the heels of his shoes.

"Five more minutes of this charade and I will," Paulette said.

She unconsciously ran her fingers through her hair, then hurriedly smoothed it down again when she realized that she was probably messing it up.

"Is it that bad?" Warren looked down at his feet when he asked.

Paulette folded her arms across her chest. "Yes, Warren, it's *that* bad."

He looked at his watch. "Well, an hour or two more and we can both head out."

"I don't think I've got even another second in me."

Warren crouched down next to her and placed a hand on her back. "They like you a lot, Paulette. They really do."

Paulette rolled her eyes. "Oh? Well, that's interesting, seeing as how they haven't even met me."

"You did great out there. That was *you* out there at that dinner table winning my parents over. That was Paulette."

She pulled at her sweater. "Nothing about *this* is Paulette. I mean, can you honestly tell me that you find me attractive in this?"

Warren cocked his head. "You're not wearing it for me."

"I'm sure as hell not wearing it for *me*."

Warren threw his hands up in surrender. "Fine, Paulette. You want to take the clothes off, go ahead. Take them off."

Paulette shrugged Warren's hands off her. "Asshole. If I had a change of clothes, I would."

Warren stood up, reached back, and turned the lock on the door. "Who needs a change of clothes?"

"Well, do you think I'm gonna walk out there naked? Or maybe have dessert with your parents in my bra and panties?" Paulette leaned forward on the toilet seat, propping her elbows on her knees.

"That's not what I'm saying." Warren's voice had become deep, his words came out slowly. "Take it off."

He moved closer, was so close to her now that Paulette could feel the heat from his body. She stood up, somehow thinking that being on her feet would give her more control.

Warren continued toward her and backed her up against the sink. Her ass rested against the cool porcelain.

"Here? You're honestly telling me you want to fuck me right here in your parents' bathroom, Warren?"

Warren's expression was unchanged. "I believe I am." Then he licked his lips. Ran his fingers lightly across her neck. Leaned down, pushed her sweater aside, and sucked on her shoulder.

And just like that, her skirt came off. The sweater followed. The awful flats dangled off her feet and fell to the floor. Paulette reached for the clasp on her bra, but Warren stopped her.

"No, stay like that," he said, "just like that. Yeah. That's my Paulette."

Warren squeezed her breasts through the satin of her bra. He slipped his fingers beneath the crotch of her panties. He kept his shirt and jacket on, his trousers up. He unzipped his fly and his cock sprang free.

He lifted Paulette by her waist and put her on the sink. His hands on her hips, he urged her forward.

Paulette wrapped her legs around his waist. She pulled and held him close.

Warren fucked her in short, quick thrusts, plunging deep now and then. She dug her nails into his cinnamon skin. She gently bit his neck and licked his earlobes.

It took Warren five minutes flat to get her off, two more to get there himself.

He was panting by the time he was done, his breath coming fast and heavy. He straightened his clothes and washed his hands.

"I'll go back out first," he said. "You clean up and join us in a few."

Warren slipped his tongue into her mouth. He brushed his hand across her wet cunt before he walked out.

— 87 —

Paulette bent down to pick up her clothes. The skirt and sweater were heavy in her hands. She brushed away the wrinkles, picked off the stray lint.

She held the clothes against her half-naked frame, looked at herself in the bathroom mirror.

No. This wasn't her at all, and it would be a lie to put it back on. Something had to be done.

Paulette began opening and shutting drawers in the Vaughns' bathroom until she found what she was looking for. From the third drawer, she retrieved a pair of scissors.

She fixed the sweater first, cutting off the sleeves at the shoulders. She cut a plunging V at the neck.

The skirt was next. She cut away what seemed like yards of fabric until what was left was a corduroy mini with a jagged hem.

Paulette put the clothes back on, pleased with the way they fit her now. The outfit suited her. The shoes, though—nothing could be done about those, so she left them where they were.

She splashed water on her face, put some on her hair and pulled her fingers through it until it gave in, bouncing back against her scalp in tight, wet curls.

Paulette opened the door and stepped out, walking barefoot into the dining room in her new outfit. The breeze against her now-exposed legs and arms snapped her awake.

She paused.

Then she walked on.

Maybe Paulette would never be the type of girl that guys like Warren could take home to their parents, and maybe that was just fine.

But for now, she took her seat at the dinner table, extended her hand to his mother, and said, "Good evening, Mrs. Vaughn, I'm Paulette, and I'm *very* pleased to meet you."

MICHELLE HOUSTON

A LONG-HELD FANTASY

DARLENE'S GUIDE TO SPICING UP YOUR SEX LIFE

    1. Food is fun to play with.

    2. Think "bondage of love."

    3. You need a spanking, you naughty girl!

    4. Sensual massage and candlelight are not antique concepts.

    5. Create a buzz with battery-operated toys.

    6. Dressing up doesn't necessarily mean going out.

Andrea paused as she reached number 6. Now *there* was an idea she hadn't considered in a long time. Skimming to the end of the article, she found the author's suggestions for roles to act out.

Be a mistress to his slave, a captive to his pirate, a schoolgirl to his principal. This isn't a movie, so it doesn't have to be fancy. Focus on the fantasy itself, instead.

Her mind already running wild with the scenario she wanted to act out, Andrea grabbed her purse and keys and headed out the door. She had less than three hours before her husband and their roommate came home from work, and she had a whole slew of errands to run.

A little more than two hours later, she pulled into the driveway and popped the trunk. After grabbing the bags from the costume store, the grocery store, and the adult shop out near the interstate, she hurried inside to set the stage. She was about to act out her secret fantasy. She was breathless already at the thought.

After a quick shower, she donned her outfit and set about turning the master bedroom into a fantasy setting, perfect for the trio to play in. She carefully draped several of her silk scarves over the bedside lamps, casting a softer glow about the room. Satin throw pillows replaced the normal bed pillows. The bed sheet and blanket were tossed into the closet, leaving only the bottom sheet. She had just finished setting the tray of fruit and wine on the nightstand when she heard her husband's car in the driveway. Grabbing her last prop, she hurried down the hall to the entryway and dropped to her knees just as the door opened.

"Honey, we're…what the hell?" Ryan's husky voice sent a shudder of sensual awareness through her. Ever since he had started dating her husband and then moved in with them, Ryan had been a part of their lives, both sexual and not. He had become her best friend, her greatest ally, and the second love of her life.

Holding out the printed paper she had rolled up and tied with a ribbon, she winked at Ryan. With a grin, he stepped aside for Daniel.

"Someone's feeling playful," Ryan said, reaching down for the scroll. Holding it out to her husband, he winked back at her.

Andrea could feel Daniel's eyes trailing over her for a moment before he pulled the paper from the ribbon and started reading aloud.

Please accept this slave as an offer of friendship between our two nations.
She has been well trained in the fine arts of pleasing a man, and it is my fondest hope that she brings you pleasure.

His voice soft and teasing, Ryan commented, "Ah, a new concubine to add to my harem." Andrea allowed herself a slight smile as Ryan continued to play along. "Let's see how well trained she truly is."

With an arrogant wave of his hand, he motioned for both of them to follow him into the bedroom. Gracefully gaining her feet, Andrea waited until Daniel moved past her. The silk of her genie costume's pants rustled slightly as she walked slowly, giving the men time to get settled. The tiny bells on the anklet she wore jingled with each step.

As she walked into the room, she found Ryan already on the bed, reclining against the pillows. Daniel joined him, leaning back against his chest. The tray of food had been moved to the bed, and while she stood there, awaiting their instructions, she watched as Daniel slowly fed Ryan a plump, ripe strawberry.

"Dance for us."

Andrea bit back a smile. The only thing Ryan liked more than watching her dance was watching her go down on her husband. She was glad she had taken the time to factor in his fantasy fetish. Crossing the room to the stereo, she pushed PLAY on the CD player. This was the kind of music she could imagine as background music in a harem. Slow, deep, and foreign, the music had a seductive quality all its own.

She lifted her hands over her head and slowly rotated her wrists, then softly thrust her hips. The bells attached to her costume's belt jingled. Her nipples tightened against her silk top, straining against the thin material. Sleeveless and ending at her midriff, the blouse covered her in the style of a bikini top, leaving most of her stomach exposed. Her pants rode low on her hips. With the predatory way that Ryan watched her movements, she felt like a true harem girl, dancing for her master. Her only goal was to please him.

As she continued to dance, Ryan's hands absently started caressing Daniel's chest, unbuttoning his shirt and pulling the tails free of his slacks. Her husband's smooth chest was slowly bared. Andrea drank in his fair skin and lanky frame. Even after years together, his body turned her on. She looked at Ryan next.

He was the definition of gorgeous, with rich chocolate eyes, a deep sun-kissed skin tone, and hands big enough to hold both a woman's wrists in one hand while he slowly fucked her senseless. Yet he had a sharp mind behind his brown eyes that tended to surprise everyone. Quick to laugh, he was even quicker to passion, which was what had first drawn Daniel to him—that quicksilver flash of lust when they first shook hands at work.

Losing herself in the fantasy, Andrea slowly turned around, rotating her waist to show off her ass. She shimmied her hips, setting the tiny bells on her body a-jingle. Across the room Daniel groaned. Glancing over her shoulder, she saw that Ryan had unzipped Daniel's pants and was slowly stroking his cock.

"Come here, slave." Ryan's voice betrayed his growing arousal.

Andrea stopped dancing and glided across the room. Climbing onto the bed, she knelt beside Ryan's hip.

"Take my other slave into your mouth."

Obediently, she licked her lips, leaned down, and kissed Daniel's cock head. He moaned softly as he thrust up against her, his fingers sliding through her hair. Her lips pressed tight around him, Andrea sucked his length into her mouth, relaxing her throat to take all of him.

"Mmm, that's good. You have been trained well."

Sucking harder, she worked his cock slowly in and out of her mouth. Her pussy growing wet against her costume, she tightened her thighs, trying to glide the damp material against her pussy. She could feel her husband's cock pulsing in her mouth as his climax approached. She wiggled her hips again, trying to generate friction on her clit.

A sharp slap against her ass stopped her movements. She jerked back in shock, her gaze meeting Ryan's. A twinkle lit his brown eyes.

"Enough of that. You move when I tell you to move and not before." He unzipped his own pants and freed his cock. "Now let's see how good a cocksucker you really are."

Daniel slid to the side as she leaned down to take Ryan's cock into her mouth. She loved its girth. Teasing him, she nipped lightly at the head before sliding down, engulfing him in the velvet heat of her mouth. He pulsed against her tongue as his hands fisted in her hair, almost ruthlessly guiding her up and down. The bells around her waist tinkled with each motion of her body as Andrea allowed her lover to guide her.

"Oh yes, I'll have to send along my thanks to your former master." Ryan's hands moved down her shoulders, pushing her away. "But for now, I wish to discover what other training you have had."

With an imperious flick of his wrist, he motioned Daniel to lie on his back. His own movements graceful, Ryan climbed off the bed and moved to stand behind her.

With his firm hands he started removing her outfit. He unzipped the top, then tossed it aside. His hands cupped her breasts, rolling the nipples between his fingers. "Take off your pants."

Her hands shaky with desire, Andrea slowly lifted her hips and pulled her pants down to her knees. Angling to her side, she pulled first one leg free, then the other. All that remained was the belt around her waist and her matching anklet. As she leaned forward, she wiggled her ass, drawing Ryan's gaze to the butt plug she had inserted before their arrival.

"Perfect," he drawled, his voice deep and husky. Andrea trembled in response as his hands glided over her ass, caressing her. "Mount my slave."

Daniel's eyes widened as she slowly crawled over him. Fully dressed, he lay passively beneath her as she gripped his cock and slowly thrust down, driving him into her pussy. His hips thrust as she squeezed tight, her body begging for more. Ryan's hands continued to caress her body as she slowly rode Daniel, her hips rocking back and forth, grinding against his pelvis.

Ryan's deft movements pulled the plug from her ass, and even before she had time to mourn the loss, he was kneeling behind her and thrusting hard past her tight ring.

"Oh God!" she gasped as he pushed his cock into her. Although she had enjoyed Daniel's cock there, it wasn't something Ryan had ever tried to do to her. Now as his girth stretched her, she tried to pull away, but Daniel's body held her pinned. There was nowhere she could go.

His hands gently against her hips, he pulled her back tighter against him, seating his cock in her ass up to the balls. Daniel thrust up against her, and Andrea whimpered at the intense sensation of two cocks within her.

The bells around her waist sounded with each stroke as Ryan slowly began to fuck her, his larger frame dwarfing hers as he pushed down against her husband, positioning her for his deep thrusts. It was everything she had fantasized about from the moment the article sparked her interest—being taken by both her men, fucked and filled by them both at the same time. She was their slave, helpless to do anything but enjoy their claiming. Her pussy ached, as she clenched tight. Behind her, Ryan groaned. "Do it again."

Already breathing hard, Andrea squeezed her pussy and ass tight, milking both cocks within her.

Ryan's hands tightened on her hips, as he started pounding against her. Beneath her, Daniel's thrusts fell into a rhythm. Now, rather than one thrusting as the other withdrew, they both thrust together. It was enough to make her scream. The tray of fruit hit the floor as the headboard started slamming against the wall under the force of their movements.

Beneath her, Daniel was thrashing slightly. With a soft grunt his orgasm washed over him, his come a warm rush in her pussy. Behind her Ryan doubled his efforts, his cock thrusting hard within her ass.

Moving a hand from her waist, he started playing with her clit, pinching the little nub between his fingers as she pressed against him. Low moans escaped her lips as she ground down against Daniel's softening cock. His eyes flickered open and met hers, and with a slight grin, he cupped her breasts and pinched her nipples roughly.

Andrea shuddered as Ryan's fingers tightened on her clit until a tidal wave of pain rushed over her, radiating out from her pussy and nipples. With a husky cry she came, collapsing against her husband. Behind her, Ryan pulled out of her ass and she felt warm spurts of come landing on her back. His hands firm, he rubbed his come into her skin, while she lay there trying to regain her breath. Sliding to the side, she curled against Daniel as Ryan shifted on the bed, moving to lie spooned against her back.

"Where on earth did you get the idea for this, baby doll?" Ryan asked a few moments later, his hands caressing little circles on her thigh.

She smiled, self-consciously. "I was reading an article about role-playing and dress-up, and I remembered those romances I read during my late teens. My favorites were the ones set in harems, where a captive woman is turned into a pleasure slave by a domineering master. They never got into too much detail, but they were enough to get me hot then."

"Mmm," Ryan breathed against her neck, "I definitely wouldn't mind acting this one out again in greater detail."

Daniel's chest rumbled under her cheek as he chuckled. "Neither would I. But next time, *you* get to be the other slave. She almost sucked me off, but then you made her quit."

SHANNA GERMAIN

PUSS-IN-BOOTS

FOUND THEM BY ACCIDENT. I'd given up the search, days and days, maybe a week ago even. Then, the night before his birthday, there they were, in the window of a second-hand store: the boots. Knee-high, black leather with at least a five-inch heel. Even through the window glass, I could tell the leather was that soft, stretchy kind, something with enough give to slide over my muscled calves. I leaned in closer to the window, put one hand up to block out the glare from the street lamp. The toes were long, but not pointed. Jesus, they were perfect, just what my husband had asked for. I'd been so sure I wasn't going to find these boots that I'd already bought him an expensive back-up gift. Who cared? I'd been given a last-minute blessing and I wasn't about to turn it away.

When I exhaled, my breath fogged up the glass, and I realized I'd been leaning in so close my nose was almost against the window.

I wanted to wipe away the fog, keep my eyes on the boots. I had a sudden fear that someone was already inside, getting ready to buy them. Or that I would walk in and the salesperson would say, "Sorry, only for show," and then I would have to get down on my hands and knees and beg her, offer her anything, *anything*, for those boots. Maybe she'd just let me borrow them for the night.

The door didn't open at first, and there was a fresh fear that I hadn't thought of, that they'd be closed already, that I would spend the night kicking myself for leaving work too late. But then I pushed instead of pulled and the door swung open to the smell of incense and patchouli and the insides of old purses.

The dark-haired girl behind the counter gave me a half-smile, just the corners of her lips U-ing up. Normally, she was the kind of girl I would had stayed and flirted with—cute in an almost boyish way, funny, great smile. But I had other things on my mind.

"Those boots," I blurted, pointing to the window. "Are they for sale?"

The girl smiled again, this time for real, showing off small, perfectly straight teeth.

"Everything's for sale," she said. "Well, except for me." She paused, seemed to think on her answer. "Well, at least not usually."

Something flooded through my stomach. "Thank God," I said. "I'll take them."

She hesitated, tucked a dark curl behind her ear. "Don't you want to know how much? Or the size or anything?"

I shook my head. It didn't matter. If they were size six, I'd pop a couple of aspirin ahead of time and squeeze my feet into them for a few hours. Even if they cost a hundred dollars, I didn't care. I'd put it on my card. My husband was only going to turn thirty once.

She took the black boots from the window display, put them on the counter. I resisted the urge to stroke the length of the leather.

"Twenty-two bucks," she said. "Size eight."

I had to laugh. It was too good to be true. They were a little big—I wear seven and a half—but I couldn't have asked for more. I wanted to hug the girl behind the counter, but she was already looking at me like I was kind of nuts, so I just put my card on the glass and said thank you.

"My pleasure, apparently." She put two fingers on the long, thin heel of a boot, stroked it gently. "Or maybe someone else's?"

I blushed then. So obvious. She could have overcharged me by a hundred bucks and I still would have said yes, I was that desperate.

Then she wrapped the boots in tissue paper, slow and careful, without looking at me, and put them in a bag. "You come back and let me know how it turns out, okay?"

"Okay," I promised—she really was cute, with that smile—and then I took my boots home to plan.

That night, I couldn't sleep. I'd put the boots in the back of the closet, next to our toys, and the thought of them nestled there, waiting, was almost more than I could stand. I wanted to slide them on now, wake him up with one heel pressed to his thigh. But I didn't. I just watched him sleep—the little laugh lines around his eyes that were new this year, the gray hairs at his temple—and imagined what I would wear with the boots tomorrow: my wrap-around dress with nothing under it, a long button-up shirt half buttoned, nothing but a black thong and a silver necklace…

In the end, I chose the black wrap-around dress, nothing under it but me. I slid it on before he got home, tied it loosely around my waist. Then I pulled the boots up over my ankles and calves. The leather curved perfectly around my calves and stopped just below the knee. I could barely walk in the heels, but I figured it didn't matter: If I could just knock his eyes out when he walked in the door, I'd be okay. I tied my long hair up in a sexy, kind of librarian bun. Then I sat down on the bed and waited.

It wasn't long before I heard the fumble of keys as he came through the front door. "Hon?" he called.

I stood up, brushed down the back of my dress, and leaned against the wall with what I hoped was a sexy, come-hither look and not a these-heels-are-too-high look. "In here," I said.

He came in, head down, hands focused on undoing his tie. "What's the deal with—" He lifted up his head and saw me.

"Happy birthday," I said, quick. Standing here with nothing on but boots and a dress so thin you could see the points of my nipples through it, I was nervous. What was I thinking? Surely he'd been kidding when he'd asked me to buy him boots for his thirtieth birthday. Jesus, I was nearly thirty myself, too old for knee-high boots and this sexy pose I was trying to pull off. My fingers tightened on the tie of my dress.

"Jesus," he said. His voice was breathy, like he'd been hit in the gut and was trying to talk. For some reason, that made me feel a little better, like maybe this hadn't been such a bad idea. And then I saw his eyes, the way they were darker than their usual dark, and a shiver went through me. Yes, this was what he'd been asking for.

Those dark eyes were silent on me so long that my thighs broke out in goose bumps all the way up to my cunt. The combination of nervous and excited had me shivering. I was afraid my teeth would chatter if he waited any longer. I inhaled, swallowed.

"Well, unwrap me already," I said, and then had to laugh at the nervous impatience in my voice.

He didn't seem to notice, or care. He just came close enough that I could see his cat-whisker wrinkles at the corners of his eyes. His hands on my lower back were warm and strong. After he pulled me against him, he ran his hands down around the curves of my ass, saying, "Oops," the same way he used to fake-yawn and put his arm around me in movie theaters. Hands settled into the curve at the bottom of my ass, he put his mouth to my earlobe, gave it a tug with his teeth.

"What if I don't want to unwrap you?" he asked.

Those goose bumps again, everywhere on my body, like they were inside too. I leaned against him, the warmth of his chest calmed my skin, the press of his already-hard cock lit my skin back on fire. I swallowed, trying to gain some sort of control. I'd forgotten how sexy he could be when he was turned on.

"Well, if you don't unwrap me, then you can't have your present," I said.

He just held me away from him, both arms straight out and me on the ends of his hands, like I was a painting he'd just found.

"Jesus," he said. "You just look gorgeous. Those boots…"

He dropped his head and I looked where he was looking, down at the boots rising up my calves, at the contrast between the black leather and the pale skin.

"You really like them?" I asked.

In answer, he went down on his knees in front of me. I gave a second of thought to his poor knees on the wood floor, thought about reminding him that he wasn't as young as he was yesterday, but then he put his mouth right at the edge of the boot, right where the leather met my skin. He licked, half leather, half skin, warm tongue and the slight scrape of teeth around the side of my calf. My goose bumps came back, pepper all the way up my legs, my back. Beneath the thin fabric of the dress, my nipples tightened. The only thing I could say was, "Oh."

He ran his hands up one boot, then the other, his palms over each ankle and shin and calf. I've never been much of a foot person—I find hips and chests and cocks and smiles sexier than feet—but there's something about the way he caressed my skin through the leather. I could understand why people found it a turn-on.

Then he went back to kissing the spots of skin right along the edge of the boots, right in the hollow at the back of my knee. With each kiss, he slid his hand a little farther up my thigh. When he reached my cunt, his fingers slid against it, then in, easy. "You're so wet," he said. He put his mouth to my belly, wiggled the ends of his fingers inside me until I shivered. "Thought this was supposed to be *my* birthday present."

"Sorry," I said. But the way he said it, I knew he didn't mind that I was enjoying it as much as he was.

When he came up from his kneel, he slipped his fingers out and his cock inside me. He was fully hard, felt longer than usual, maybe it was the angle, and I moaned in surprise and pleasure as he made his way up. He thrust inside me, kissing my chin, my cheeks, the side of my nose, somewhere new, with each tip of his hips. In my boots, I was almost as tall as he was—I didn't have to stand on my tiptoes to meet him, it was like he was lifting me up, balancing me on his cock.

He slid out of me. "Let's get on the bed," he said. "I can't see your boots from here."

He undressed fast, a kid with a present in front of him, unable to slow down. Then, he climbed on the bed, lay down on his back with his hands behind his head. I almost laughed—lying that way, he was all cock, the way it stuck up away from his body, that sweet curve toward his belly that I loved.

I reached down, started to peel the boots down.

"No, please," he said. "Leave them on."

"What about the bedspread?"

"Do I look like I care?" he asked.

And gazing at him, lying there naked, cock up and waiting for me, I realized that I didn't care either. I climbed onto the bed and straddled him, keeping the boots as close to his hips as I could, so he would feel the leather every time I moved. I found his cock with my hand and squatted over him, my thighs already starting to ache. But I didn't care, it was worth it to feel him inside me like this.

I slid myself slowly down over his cock, taking him in, little bit by little bit, loving the way his eyes closed and his mouth opened. He didn't make much of a sound until I grabbed his shoulders, used the leverage to lift myself up and down on his cock. Then he moaned, his head back a little, and he reached out and grabbed the boots at the ankles. The feel of his hands through the leather made my cunt ache like it was empty even though he was already inside me.

"Want to switch?" he asked after a few minutes. And I did, but I didn't. My thighs burned from holding myself over him, but everything else was burning too, in a good way. Then I remembered, this was his birthday. Not mine.

"Do you?" I asked. He pumped his hips up into me a few times, hard and quick, his eyes closed.

"Let's switch," he said. "I need a condom anyway."

While he grabbed one from the dresser, I rolled over on the bed, so that when he turned back around I was all ass and boots. He didn't even stop to put the condom on—just put his hands around the sides of my ass, slid himself back into me.

"Jesus," he said. "You're killing me."

"Well, you're old enough now to have an insurance policy, so maybe I am," I said.

Instead of responding, he thrust into me harder, which is what I knew he'd do. I leaned back into his thrusts. I love that position, the way his balls slap against me, the way he reaches around, like now, to find my nipples, tweak them.

"Bitch," he said, and he dropped his hand off my nipple and put his finger right on my clit.

"Shit." My voice was mostly breath and push, the sharp inhale of pleasure.

After a second, he dropped his finger away and pulled out of me. I moaned, aching from lack. I heard the sound of the condom wrapper and felt him pushing back into me, different now, but just as hard, just as much him.

And then he wrapped his hands around the ankles of the boots, lifted them up. For a second, it was like a new yoga pose—doggy-style with boots. But then my hips settled in, and I could push back into him. His hands tightened around my ankles with each thrust.

"You're going to have to get yourself off," he said. At first I didn't understand, but then I realized he meant because his hands were full. I went down on one shoulder, pushing my ass even further in the air, and reached down with one hand. My clit was huge and wet, and as soon as I touched it, it sent shivers through me. I felt kind of bad, because it was his birthday, and I was the one getting myself off.

But then he said, "Go ahead," and I realized it was good for him too, feeling me finger myself while he was inside me. I rubbed my clit hard while he fucked me, thought about him behind me, his hands tight around my ankles. I came before he did, but it was okay, because when he came, he came a long time, shuddering into me, dropping the boots and leaning over my back like he couldn't hold himself up. His heart pounding against my back, matching the pumping of my own heart and clit.

"Jesus," he said against my back. "Jesus, Jesus."

I laughed, and gave him a bit of a shove so he'd start moving. He did, and I rolled over and pulled off the boots. He watched me from the bed, his cock still wrapped in the condom.

"I'm not even going to ask where you found those boots," he said.

I lay down beside him, our bodies only warmth and skin and sweat.

"I had to trade my soul for them."

He snuggled up to my neck.

"Hmm," he said. "It was well worth it."

"I hope so," I said. "Happy birthday, baby."

When he laughed, I saw the new lines around his mouth too, little smile echoes.

"Yes, it is." Then he sighed. "This morning I felt old."

"And now?"

"Now, not so much."

"Good," I said.

"Plus," he said, putting his hands into my hair, and kissing my chin, "you're catching up. Next month, you'll be as old as me. And, I have no idea what you're going to ask for, but I highly doubt you can top those boots."

I rolled over and moved closer to him, so I could feel his heartbeat against my back again. I thought of the girl behind the counter, her short dark hair and playful eyes, the way she'd smiled when she'd wrapped up the boots. "Oh, I'm sure I'll think of something," I said.

TSAURAH LITZKY

LIPSTICK

WAYNE WAS IN THE KITCHEN making coffee. "Listen," he called in to me, "come to my place for dinner Saturday. I'll make my specialty, linguine and clam sauce."

"Your *specialty?*" I called back. "It's the only dish you know how to make. You should buy stock in Progresso."

"Don't spend my money for me," he said, laughing.

"Why not?" I countered. "You know I'll eat all your linguine."

After he left, I just wanted to stay in bed wrapped in the odors of sex that scented the sheets. I couldn't believe my luck: a decent, zany, fuck wizard who wrote stories and plays, had a job, *and* knew how to cook. Also, he liked everything about me, even the way my tits had started to hang low on my chest. He savored them as if they were the Golden Apples of the Hesperides. He said their sexy swing turned him on.

I had to go teach my writing class, so I forced myself to get up and dress. In the mirror above the bathroom sink I looked happy. I reached for my favorite lipstick in the makeup bowl on the shelf but it wasn't there. The tube wasn't beside the faucet on the sink or in the medicine cabinet. I returned to the bedroom and checked the purse I had been carrying the previous night. I looked among my jewelry on the dresser. It wasn't anywhere, my twenty-dollar tube of Shiseido Strong Red. Rouge Formidable, it said on the label. The lipstick was gone, vanished!

It was sacrilege for me to go out without lipstick, so I colored my lips with an old tube of Tangerine Tango that made me look like a refugee from a shuffleboard court in Miami, and then I went out the door.

All week long, I searched for the Rouge Formidable. I was bereft without it. It was the perfect shade of red to bring out the gold in my brown eyes, the tawny olive tint of my skin. I always wore lipstick; I felt naked if I faced the world with none on.

I can trace my love of lipstick to my mother. It was the only cosmetic she ever wore, and she was so beautiful, inside and out. When I was sixteen, she took me to the Woolworth's to buy me my first lipstick. After trying on at least ten shades, we finally settled on a vibrant Petunia Pink. My mother bought it for ninety-nine cents. Then she showed me how to put it on, tracing the outline of my lips first and then filling in. She pulled a Kleenex from her purse, saying, "Always blot your lipstick, it locks in the color," then handing the tissue to me. I followed her instructions. "Look at yourself now," she said. In the mirror above the lipstick display, I looked stunning. I was no longer a geeky high school girl. I was a babe. I looked like a movie star, a glamorous femme fatale.

Eventually, I found out there was much more to being a femme fatale than knowing how to paint my lips Petunia Pink. I learned that men like to be told how big and strong they are, and it helps if you can mix a good drink. I learned miraculous tricks with push-up bras and garter belts. Even more important, I discovered that discretion is the better part of fidelity, particularly since I didn't like to sleep alone.

I learned how very fundamental it is to know when to say *yes* and when to say *no*. This has always been the most difficult for me. I've found myself saying yes when I should say no so often, I'm not sure I could ever qualify as a bona fide femme fatale. But since I've been with Wayne, I don't care. I feel safe.

He never laughs at what I have to say. He loves my chatterbox ways. In bed he can be a combination of Yojimbo and Evel Knievel, yet it doesn't seem to matter to him whether he isn't always on top. When I want to take control, he just gives it up and gets into it. Last night, he stripped me in the kitchen, undressed himself, then led me to bed. He spanked my big bottom not all that lightly with my old Ping-Pong paddle from Camp Lokanda until my ass was throbbing and stinging and singing his name. Then, so as not to stress my tender butt, we fucked doggy-style. Afterward, we rested spoon-style—him curled up behind me, his arm over my shoulder, his hand cradling my breast.

I was still feeling feisty, so I soon put my head between his legs. I washed his family jewels with my tongue and got him all wet and juicy. I started pulling on his fat, purple cock, but he didn't complain. I slapped it and it reared right up like a bucking bronco so I slapped it again.

"Hit me some more," he said, and I did, more than once, but I didn't want to spoil him, so I stopped. Holding that frisky bronc in my hand, I bent my head again and my tongue found its way to his tender back hole and fucked him there. Soon he was jerking his hips, moaning and calling my name. When I was ready to take him and break him, I pushed him back flat on the bed. I straddled his hips, hovered over his splendid organ, and then, taking him deep into my cunt all the way, I galloped that big horse home.

By the time Saturday night came along, I still hadn't found my lipstick. I found a tube of Revolution Ruby that would have to do, but it just wasn't as bright as Rouge Formidable. I'd have to buy another tube. I set off for Wayne's place in Williamsburg.

I liked his apartment. Unlike mine, it was always sparkling clean. The walls were painted a rich gold. Ivy and red-and-white begonias flourished in pots on the windowsills.

He answered the door so quickly I thought he must have been listening for my step on the stairs.

"Come in, come in," he said, and put his arm around me, pulling me inside. I handed him the Chianti I had brought. "Thanks," he said, "Perfect choice," then, "I'm still cooking. Let me pour you some of this to drink. "

He led me into the kitchen. He uncorked the wine and poured some into a juice glass with little oranges on it. When he gave it to me, I kissed his hand "thank you" and went into the other room. I wandered over to his writing table. Through the window above the table I could see the low roofs of factories and industrial buildings topped by an occasional water tower.

A stack of papers sat next to the computer. The first page was titled *Satan's Sex Change,* the new play he was working on. He had told me about it and I was curious, but I didn't want to look at it without being invited. Maybe he'd read part of it to me later. I sat down on his bed and kicked off my shoes, inadvertently knocking over the little wastebasket beside the bed. When I bent over to right it, the stink of cigarettes slapped me in the face. The only thing I didn't like about him was that he was a heavy smoker.

The butts in the basket were ringed with a bright, bright red. *What is this?* I thought—*a visiting friend, a cousin, his mother?* Whoever she is, she smokes his brand. I suddenly felt upset, but why shouldn't he have a woman friend over? Was it any of my business? Still, the very first time he put his hand between my legs he yelled joyously, "Mine, mine, mine."

I had answered, "Okay, but it has to be reciprocal." He assured me that would be fine.

"Absolutely, no problem," he said.

So why were these butts in the wastebasket that was right next to the bed? Why weren't they in the garbage pail under the sink in the kitchen? Who had smoked them down?

My hands were suddenly clammy, my head ached. I was feeling crazy. How could he two-time me when it was so good between us? *I can't bear sharing,* I thought, *but maybe it really was his mother. I'll never know if I don't ask.*

I put the glass of Chianti down on the floor beneath the bed and picked up one of the butts with the lipstick tattoo. Then I marched into the kitchen, holding it in front of me like a tiny sword. He was standing, humming "Lay, Lady, Lay" at the sink, rinsing the linguine in a colander.

"Look," I said, brandishing the butt in front of him, "there's lipstick on this. If you're seeing someone else, tell me straight out. I can't stand deception, I can't handle it."

He turned to me, and the humming stopped. His face paled, suddenly as white as the linguine in the colander.

"It's not that, no…it's not w-wh—," he stammered, "what you think." He turned the water off, put the colander down.

"So what is it, then?" I asked sharply.

"I w-w-w-wanted to tell you, I was going to tell you, I knew I h-h-h-had to…" he stuttered.

He looked so upset that my heart opened to him. I wanted to take him in my arms, but then I remembered how I'm always saying yes when I should be saying no. I made myself step back, but then he reached out and grabbed my wrist roughly. He pulled me with surprising force across the floor to his closet and jerked open the door. He reached into the back of the closet and pulled out an armful of garments—a bunch of dresses. He threw them on the bed. There was a large, long, chartreuse strapless evening dress—very dowdy; a few gaudy, flowered cotton house dresses; a beige silk shirtwaist dress with a full skirt. Then he stooped and gathered up some shoes from the bottom of the closet—big red suede pumps; black stiletto spiked heels; a pair of silver flats. He threw the shoes on top of the dresses.

"See, see," he bellowed, "I'm a transvestite! Now you know. I have to tell you, please believe me, I need to tell you I'm not gay, I don't want to go with men."

For once, I was speechless. I had lost my voice in the black abyss yawning at my feet. I found myself thinking that the chartreuse evening dress was made of the cheapest, tackiest rayon and had too many pleats, and the floral patterns on the housedresses were ugly and overworked. As a transvestite, he had lousy taste.

Finally I managed to say, "You're a wonderful person, you're great in bed, so what if you're also attracted to men? Besides, everyone is really attracted to their own sex as well as the opposite sex, but most people just lie about it."

"No, no, no, it's n-n-n-n-ot ab-b-bout sex, "he spat out, "and I don't want to go to bed with other men, or women either. I want *you*, you're the one."

"Just me?" I asked.

"Just you," he answered. "I love being with you. I wanted to tell you before, but I couldn't." He was trembling. He sat down on one of the two chairs, clasped his hands in his lap, and looked down and then back up at me. "I feel like a psycho sometimes," he said, "because I have to hide this. I left home after high school, started to drive a taxi. I tried to write, but didn't have the confidence. I took a few writing classes but couldn't produce a thing. Then one day when I was alone in the apartment I shared with my old girlfriend Laura, I went into the bathroom. She had left her lipstick uncapped, standing on the sink. Without thinking I reached out, picked it up, and put lipstick on my mouth for the first time. It was a vivid fuchsia color. When I looked in the mirror, I looked like a clown with a five o'clock shadow, but then, as if I was in a dream, I went back to the typewriter. In ten minutes I wrote a terrific poem about the loneliness of eagles. Soon after that, I started to cross-dress and the writing flowed. Laura couldn't take it and I couldn't hide it from her, so we broke up."

"So that's why you swiped my lipstick. It's my lipstick on the cigarette butts."

"Yeah, of course," he said.

Now I was totally overwhelmed, shocked. I heard myself saying, "Certainly you could afford your own. I've been going crazy looking for that lipstick. It's the most expensive one I've ever owned, a twenty-dollar lipstick, twenty-two if you count the tax."

"Sure, sure, I could afford my own but I couldn't help myself. I took it because it was yours, your very special lipstick. I thought it would inspire me… I-I-I love you."

I felt like bolting out the door. So *this* is what I attract—the first man in five years who can keep my fuse lit, and he wants to dress up like Doris Day! But then I heard the voices of the many true gods speaking in my head: *So what?* they said, *no one is perfect.*

I thought about the boyfriend before Wayne, the one who always had to be on top. I thought about the one before that, the one who dropped me when he found out how old I was. I remembered how lonely I was before I met Wayne, how desolate. I leaned over and put my hand on his knee.

"Put on one of the dresses," I said, "and the lipstick."

"What?" he asked in disbelief. "Why, do you want to laugh at me?"

"No—no, silly," I said. "Maybe I only want to look at your legs."

He lifted his head, looked at me shyly, with a tentative, please-like-me smile, and I grinned right back. He went to the bed and picked up the chartreuse evening dress. I couldn't repress a shudder.

"Not that one. Any one but that one, please." I said. He grabbed one of the housedresses and vanished into the bathroom, slamming the door.

When he opened the bathroom door and stepped back into the room, his clear blue eyes were accented with black eyeliner. It was crooked and smudged, so it looked like he had dirt all around his eyes. He had also put on some peachy-pink blusher that clashed with his fair complexion. My Rouge Formidable was slathered too thickly over his lips. He was easily the handsomest man I had ever seen.

"You're gorgeous," I told him, "so hot that my pussy is beginning to steam."

The housedress he had chosen was patterned with dark blue and green flowers; the dress was much too short for his six-foot frame. The bottom button of the dress was undone and the tip of his long, pink cock poked out between the blue and green flowers like a strange, delicate bud. Behind his cock I could see the purple globes of his balls. I had never wanted to suck a cock so much in my life. The way the dress opened over it made me think of the chuppah, the ceremonial canopy the bride and groom stand under during a Jewish marriage ceremony. I wanted to marry his cock. "My love is as rich with sap as a cedar in the spring," the Song of Solomon says.

I went to him, put my arms around his waist so that we were body to body. He was breathing fast and I could feel the blood coursing beneath his skin. I knelt before him. I lifted the hem of his dress so my face was in front of his magnificent set. His cock was a robust tree, his thighs a forest of strength. When I took him in my mouth I smelled that scent of cedar and pine. I ran my tongue round and round him, I sucked him deep, and the more he stiffened, the harder I sucked as he swelled even more and filled my whole mouth. I knew I could never get enough of him. I moved my hand to his balls. I wanted to caress his apples, his pomegranates, his fruits with their magic seeds. They were growing and I needed both hands to juggle them. I heard the sharp, rapid breathing that meant he was about to climax. I had to summon all my will to make my mouth release him, he was so sweet.

"Wait, wait, "I said as I stood and stripped off my clothes. "Where's my lipstick?"

He couldn't stop panting, he was so excited. "In the medicine cabinet," he gasped.

"Just wait," I said. I dashed in, got it, and returned to him. I wiped off the lipstick he had applied. "I want to make your mouth up. I've had a lot of practice."

I carefully outlined his full lips with the lipstick and then I filled the outline in.

I stepped back to look at his mouth, the most alluring mouth I had ever seen.

"Now you look so sexy, like Rudolph Valentino, King of Lovers."

He grinned, then grabbed me and kissed me, smearing my Rouge Formidable all over my lips. Then I just lay down on his hard wood floor and spread my legs. I loved how his rigid cock looked poking out of that dress. I put my hands beneath my ass and raised my hips, opening my sweet rosebud up to my lipstick love.

ALISON TYLER

EDIT ME

D AMN GOOD START," Hunter said, looking over the interview I'd
done with Flea from the Chili Peppers. "But your lead needs more
energy."

I watched as he used a bright red pen to mark my draft up, and
even though the stark white paper looked bled on when he'd finished,
I didn't say a word. Hunter was my mentor. That's what he called it.
I called it something else, but never to his face.

"Like this," he said, easily penning a new opening sentence that
throbbed with the intensity of a Chili Peppers bass line.

I nodded, awed, as always, by the effortless way he fixed my pieces.
I knew he wasn't scrawling across my paper out of spite or animosity.
After several weeks on the job, I'd learned a simple truth: Hunter was
extremely particular about the end result—whether it be for a story in
the newspaper that he owned and I wrote for, or my own appearance.

He'd adjust my lead sentence if he disagreed with a solitary word choice, and he'd adjust my bra strap when it slid free, his fingers lingering— I thought, I *hoped*—for an extra beat beneath the fine strap of silken fabric.

Surreptitiously, I observed his interactions with my fellow staff members and realized that he didn't touch the other writers the way he touched me. But I didn't know why. I'd gotten the job from a board at UCLA, a mentorship program. A way to learn about the world. I convinced myself that the extra interest he showed in me was simply because he was taking his job seriously.

"Lose the sweater," he'd say, motioning to my oversized thrift-store black cardigan with moth holes in the sleeves, grimacing as if it pained him to look at the thing. "Take out the hair ribbon. Then tie the ribbon around your neck. Like that. Perfect."

I was eighteen, out in the real world for the first time, shy and naïve. I didn't think it mattered what writers wore, but Hunter disagreed. He taught me how to dress, and he often re-dressed me when I came to work. I made the adjustments without a complaint. My goal was to please him. With my writing. With myself.

Edit me, I thought every time I entered the office. *Edit me.*

He was my mentor, and he bought me things.

Like The Clash's *London Calling.*

And pretty pink panties with polka dots.

And high-heeled Mary Janes when he got tired of my favorite pair of battered black Docs Martens that I wore daily, regardless of the occasion. In my defense, the setting was an alternative art-house weekly where fashion was far more *bizarre* than *Bazaar*. Our photography editor,

Pryor McNicols, wore Elvis Costello–style geek glasses and bowling shirts featuring other people's names: Biff, Carlos, Ned. Our music editor sported a bright-blue Mohawk, which looked good with her cobalt eyes. The tough ex-con in charge of collecting advertising payments boasted full-arm tattoos of naked '40s-style pinups. But even with the artsy set, wearing Docs with everything from plaid micro-miniskirts to short black dresses was pushing the fashion factor past the breaking point.

"Try them," he said softly when I opened the shoe box after work. "Just try them on—"

I sat down on the floor to undo the laces of my boots, and Hunter watched patiently from the edge of his desk, his head cocked as I finally slid on the patent leather shoes he'd chosen and buckled them over the ankle.

"Better," he said, smiling as I did my best not to tip over. "Now, you look like a grown-up."

Hunter's mother was from Japan, his father from Denmark, and he'd wound up with exotic, almost unreasonable good looks. Tall and handsome, he had the strongest jaw you could imagine, cheekbones like cut glass, and glossy black shoulder-length hair that I longed to run my fingers through. He dated girls who were models or starlets— lean and sleek, like cats in the wild, with golden manes and chestnut skin. I couldn't have been more different. I'm slim and pale with dark hair and dark eyes, and at the time I had "goth girl" written all over me. Hunter said I was hiding—the way the best portions of my stories were buried beneath extra words. My looks were similarly hampered by the ill-fitting clothes I favored. But black made me feel safe, and my Docs made me invincible.

With his wealth and his exotic looks, Hunter could have had almost any girl he chose, but that summer he took me for lunch each day, and he told me things. Taught me things. While we ate our meals I tried my best to emulate the model girls he dated.

Editors—good editors—are by nature freaks for control. Hunter was no different. He needed to have his whole staff in place the way he desired. We worked for him, so that made sense. But with me, he took things further. Beyond deadlines. Beyond lead sentences. He was sexy with me, leaning across the table at lunch and saying in a low, soft voice, "I held her hands together over her head. Stretching her. I kept hold of her wrists as I fucked her and she couldn't get free."

My panties, newly purchased, perfectly polka dot, were drenched. I squirmed, and he admonished me. "You flush so prettily. It's lovely with your pale skin. But you shouldn't squirm around as if you're uncomfortable. You should soak it all in when a man tells you secrets. You should learn from what he says."

Soak. That was a good word. That's what I did.

"Now ask," he'd say magnanimously, lifting his emerald green bottle of imported beer to his lips. "Ask whatever you want."

He was fair in that way, always allowing me to quiz him after the lunchtime lessons. I tried to show him that I was learning, that I'd paid attention and memorized the facts. But I wasn't used to drinking beer during the day, stolen sips I took from his bottle. My mind felt hazy around the edges, and all I could mumble was, "Did she like it?"

A headshake.

A frown.

I'd asked the wrong question, and I felt as bad as if he'd put me over his lap and spanked me. No, that's a lie. Because that's what I *wished* he would do. I hated to disappoint him. I wanted to make him proud. This was why I spent hours agonizing over the leads in my sentences, as well as the clothes in my closet.

"Did she come?" I asked.

That was better. More in-your-face, which he liked coming from me. I was so desperately quiet, so curiously shy. How'd I get like that? He simply couldn't fathom. I was no L.A. woman, true. A transplanted San Francisco girl, I couldn't begin to blend in a world of silicone and faux blondes. With my pale skin, dark-cherry lips, and long dark curly hair, I didn't fit in. Hunter liked that. He wanted me to blush less, but be comfortable more. Confidence, he said, was power.

"Of *course* she came."

And then, to show him that I was advancing, that I was finally catching on, I said in as husky a voice as I could manage, "I would have come, too."

His smile lit his face. He had perpetual smudges underneath his dark, almost-purple-blue eyes. The signs of fatigue proved that he ran the newspaper from dawn till dawn. He might have been wealthy, but he wasn't a party boy. He got his hands dirty. And oh, did I want those dirty hands around *my* wrists. Holding *me* down. Stretching *me*. Not letting me free. Not even for a second.

When I came out of the ladies' room after touching up my makeup, he smeared my lipstick with the ball of his thumb, so that my lips looked freshly kissed and viper-stung. I imagined sucking his thumb, if only he'd let me. Imagined sucking his cock, on my knees in his office, showing him that I was an apt pupil, if only he'd let me.

He said he was my mentor.

I called him something else entirely. But not to his face.

"He's a misogynist," my ultrafeminist best friend said when I confessed my crush. "Who gives a staff member shoes?" (I didn't tell her about the rest. About the way he re-dressed me, about his thumb on my bottom lip.) "He wants to shape you. Change you. Break you," Shanna insisted.

But I didn't think of Hunter in the same way. He was my editor. He wanted to *edit* me. I was made of good raw material, but I needed a firm hand to guide me. My fantasies went far deeper than that. I craved scarlet lines marking my pale skin, echoes of his red pen on my rough drafts. *I* was a rough draft. I needed a fierce lead.

Late at night, after we put the paper to bed, I wished that he would put me to bed. Once back in my 1940s-style apartment on Malcolm and Wilshire, I'd stay awake in my tiny twin, staring at the cracks in the ceiling, and I'd remember each lesson. Hunter said he was my mentor, but I thought of him as my master. As someone who could own me. Who could turn me into the type of wild-jaguar-girls that he squired around to the best restaurants in town. As the summer progressed, I watched, and I learned. I stayed at the office until the stars came out. My writing improved until he hardly had to use that pen at all. Each lunchtime, I listened to Hunter's stories, and I felt as though I was starting to understand the language he wanted me to learn. I grew bolder. I asked the right questions. I wore the right shoes.

On the last day of my summer job, I straightened my hair. I even got a spray-on tan, so that my skin was golden, gleaming. I slid on those high-heeled shoes—I had learned to walk in them after hours of practice. Not toe-heel clomping, but heel-toe forceful, as if I knew where I was going. As if I had somewhere to go.

I showed up at work in a silky pastel wrap-around dress and my stacked-heel Mary Janes, pretending that nothing had happened. That nothing was different. Big silver hoop earrings dangled nearly to my shoulders. An exquisite perfume had been dabbed at my pulse points. I knew Hunter saw me. He had to notice. Everyone else on staff oohed and ahhed at my transformation, and I glowed inside, knowing that I'd done well. As pleased as when I turned in a perfectly polished article.

But Hunter didn't say a word.

All day long I tried to get a rise out of him.

I filed in front of him, bent over the desk the way I'd read about in a *Cosmo* how-to article. How to get a man to notice you? Bend over while filing. That was the number one suggestion. (Number two was "Spill red wine on your white shirt during an office party and dab at the stain suggestively.") I felt his eyes on me. I was thin and sleek and wildcat-like. My lips were smudged and bee-stung. My hair was still black, but my crazy-messy tousle of curls had been tamed. Now my hair was shiny as obsidian and fell straight past my shoulders to the middle of my back. And my beloved Docs were gone.

The truth was that *I* was gone. I just didn't know that. I didn't get it.

I hadn't learned a fucking thing.

For the first time all summer, Hunter didn't take me to lunch that day. He didn't say a word.

At the end of the day, once the rest of the staff had departed, Hunter locked the outer office door and came toward me. Those dark-blue eyes burned into me, so cold they were hot, and I thought I'd won. I'd done what he'd silently requested. I'd transformed myself into his type of girl. Yet I could tell from the look on his face that something had gone desperately wrong. He grabbed me by my upper arm and pulled me into his office. I felt weak-kneed, violently unsure of what was going on.

He pulled the tie at my waist, and my dress flickered opened. He slid the fabric off my body, leaving me in my polka-dot panties and matching bra. And then he bent me forward, over his desk, and he slapped my ass hard.

"You don't have to be someone else," he said ferociously into my silence.

"But I thought—" I murmured, already soaking, staring over my shoulder at him in shocked alarm. Not shocked because he'd spanked me, but shocked because I'd somehow misunderstood. After all his lessons, I'd still managed to fail.

"You thought wrong."

"But you always date the girls who—"

His firm, strong hand smacked my panty-clad ass again, and I choked my words down, understanding that this was yet another lesson, that I was back in pupil mode. My favorite place to be.

"You're perfect," he said. "The other you. The different you. This *isn't* you."

None of this made any sense to me. "I don't—"

Another loud, hard smack, and I bit my tongue to keep myself silent. I'd taken the summer internship to learn. And here I was, learning.

He spanked me hard, until I was crying, until I set my head on the cool wood of his desk and let all the tears flow out of me. And then he carried me to the expensive black leather sofa along the far wall of his office and put me over his lap, pulled down my sopping wet under-wear, and spanked me on my bare bottom. His hand slapped my right cheek, then my left, leaving me breathless and shaking. And I cried some more, cried more tears than I'd thought I had in me. I didn't try to get away from him. I stayed in place as best I could, hoping that he'd see how hard I was trying to please him. Hoping I wouldn't fail him again.

His hand came down again and again, marking me, making me his. The smacks of his firm hand reverberated in the quiet room. The sound of my breathing, of my sobs, was loud in my head. I was embarrassed by how vulnerable I felt, yet I could do nothing about it.

Afterward, he held me in his arms and let me ask, as he always did. Fair to the end. Let me ask my questions. Let me try to understand. The same way he did at lunch. The same way he did in staff meetings, when he explained what he wanted for the issue, and then let the writers duke it out.

"I don't understand—" I whispered, tears staining my cheeks, so aware that I was sitting nearly naked on his clothed lap, that I could feel his hard cock pressing up against me through his slacks, that I was leaving a damp spot right on his crotch. So aware of my burning hot skin, of the marks he'd left that I would be able to admire later. "I thought you wanted—"

"You," he said, his thumb along my bottom lip once more, and this time, I drew it in and sucked on it, as I'd always imagined. "I wanted you."

And still I didn't understand. Why hadn't he said? Why had he talked about the wild nights with the other girls all those times? I stared at him, my eyes wide, trembling in his embrace as he continued.

"I didn't know how you felt," he said. "Those mysterious dark eyes never let me in. But when I saw what you did. The dress. The hair. The tan…" He made a face.

"But you always date the sorts of girls—"

He shrugged. "Those are the only kinds of girls there are in L.A."

"That's not true," I countered, thinking of Sylvia and her blue Mohawk.

"Come on, kid," he said, "there's a cookie-cutter look in this town. All the women I meet have that same straightened hair, same model walk. It's why I take *you* to lunch everyday."

"But you always gave me advice."

"Not to change you into one of *them*," he said, sounding horrified. And I thought back and realized that he had never said a word about my hair, or about the color of my clothes. He'd merely adjusted, the way he adjusted my words, wanting cleaner lines, a tighter fit. Just like he had never demolished one of my articles, sending me back to the start. He had simply polished my writing until my words were ready for print. I closed my eyes, trying to understand, and finally got it: He hadn't wanted the goth in my world to disappear. He'd simply wanted—

"To make you more…" He hesitated now, and I opened my eyes and stared at him, seeing him search. "…More confident in being you. That's the only thing you lack. In your writing and in yourself."

That's right, I thought. He'd told me that. Confidence was power.

"And more than that, I wanted an acknowledgment that you were ready. I gave you those gifts. I took you to lunch. I was waiting."

As I'd been waiting. Staring at the cracks in my ceiling. Trying to put it all together.

"Do you understand me now?"

"Yes, sir," I whispered, moving out of his embrace and down on the floor in front of him. I set my head against his thigh, then reached to open his slacks, my lips parting to take in his cock. I would suck it all night. I would sleep with it in my mouth, like a pacifier.

He called himself my mentor, but I had another word. A different word entirely—one I could finally say to his face.

ABOUT THE EDITOR

CALLED "A TROLLOP WITH A LAPTOP" by *East Bay Express,* Alison Tyler is naughty and she knows it. Ms. Tyler is the author of more than twenty explicit novels, including *Learning to Love It, Strictly Confidential, Sweet Thing, Sticky Fingers,* and *Something About Workmen* (all published by Black Lace), as well as *Rumors, Tiffany Twisted,* and *With or Without You* (Cheek). Her novels and short stories have been translated into Japanese, Dutch, German, Italian, Norwegian, and Spanish.

Ms. Tyler's short stories in multiple genres have appeared in many anthologies as well as in *Playgirl* magazine and *Penthouse Variations.*

She is the editor of *Batteries Not Included* (Diva); *Heat Wave, Best Bondage Erotica* volumes 1 & 2, *The Merry XXXmas Book of Erotica, Luscious, Red Hot Erotica, Slave to Love, Three-Way, Happy Birthday Erotica, Caught Looking* (with Rachel Kramer Bussel), and *Got a Minute?* (all from Cleis Press); *Naughty Fairy Tales from A to Z* (Plume); and the *Naughty Stories from A to Z* series, the *Down & Dirty* series, *Naked*

Erotica, and *Juicy Erotica* (all from Pretty Things Press). Please visit www.prettythingspress.com or www.alisontyler.blogspot.com.

Ms. Tyler is loyal to coffee (black), lipstick (red), and tequila (straight). She has tattoos, but no piercings; a wicked tongue, but a quick smile; and bittersweet memories, but no regrets.

In all things important, she remains faithful to her partner of eleven years, but she still can't choose just one perfume.